My illusion my Mistake

The
Uncommitted commitment

AKSHAT JAIN

© Akshat Jain 2019

All rights reserved

All rights reserved by author. No part of this publication may be reproduced, stored in a retrieval system or transmitted in any form or by any means, electronic, mechanical, photocopying, recording or otherwise, without the prior permission of the author.

Although every precaution has been taken to verify the accuracy of the information contained herein, the author and publisher assume no responsibility for any errors or omissions. No liability is assumed for damages that may result from the use of information contained within.

Disclaimer: In this work of fiction, the characters, places, and events are either the product of the author's imagination or they are used entirely fictitiously. Any resemblance to actual persons, living or dead, is purely coincidental.

First Published in February 2020

ISBN: 978-81-945228-0-5

BLUEROSE PUBLISHERS
www.bluerosepublishers.com
info@bluerosepublishers.com
+91 8882 898 898

Cover Design:
Mohit Joshi

Typographic Design:
Namrata Saini

Distributed by: BlueRose, Amazon, Flipkart, Shopclues

Special Thanks to

My God,
My Mom & Dad

for everything

Dedicated to
My Grandfather
"Late Seth Shri Ghasi Ram Ji Jain"
&
My Uncle
"Late Sh. Vipin Kumar Jain"
From your loving Grandson & Nephew

- **Akshat Jain**

I know it hurt you;
It hurt me too,
But now that you're gone
All I know is I miss you.

You were there for so long,
I never thought you would leave.
I thought you had another year
Waiting up your sleeve.

The day that you left
Was the saddest of my life
I remember sitting at home
And crying all day and night.

I might be selfish
But I wish you were here,
Or if you stayed
For one more year.

I know you loved me,
And I still love you too.
So I'm trying to be strong
Just for you.

*I know I'm not perfect.
I know I'll never be.
I just hope you're up there
And that you're proud of me.*

*You had to let go
Even though you were holding on for so long,
But there's not a day I don't think of you
And how you were so strong.*

*I just want to tell you
That you're always in my heart.
Even though I still cry
I know we're not apart.*

Thinking of you, Grandpa...

By Amanda Dwyer

Acknowledgement

Every creation takes place due to some cause. And mine is no different. Thus, if I were to extend my gratitude to some specific set of people for making this book possible, then that would be an understatement to their contribution in my life. So, I shall try to put it this way: Have you seen a garland made of pearls? It is a series of pearls knitted together. One cannot do without the other. In that same manner, I cannot even do without a single pearl of my life.

The very first letter of this book was penned down because of one of the pearl of my life. It is someone without her mistakes & flying desire, this book would have never come into existence. Thus, I am thankful for the twists and turns that life brought along with it and gave me so much to learn. Next up, I would like to mention God for giving me such a wonderful family and an incredible opportunity to actually express the ripples of my heart in form of words. To my beloved wife, Manisha, who stood as an enormous pillar in my life and helped me through the tough times like a trustworthy companion. I consider myself blessed with such great parents and an incredible set of friends who have always been there for me, no matter what.

Two of my friend deserve special mention for their continued support throughout the process. Chetan Bhatt working with one of the leading IT company, he gave me valuable inputs in this project. Wing Commander Deepak

Yadav who reviewed the work thoroughly and gave me candid opinions on the script and design. And yes one more, Sohan Show who is currently studying in undergrad at Massachusetts Institute of Technology, United States, He advised me many a times about the content and the write-up of this book

I also extend my heartiest thanks to Prof. Satya Bhushan Das and Prof. Venkat-IIM Lucknow- who taught me how to view a particular thing as a bigger picture and express it in my own words. I also cannot do without mentioning the following dignitaries: General Bipin Rawat, Grp Captain Anupam Banerjee (PRO Indian Air Force, South Block, Ministry of Defence), Grp. Captain A K Charodia (Retd.) & DIG N C Jhingta (Ministry of Home Affairs) who all inspired me on various occasions & ceremonies and also gave me the chance to discuss critical matters with them.

When we ventured into the world of writing, we had heard many a horrifying tale of first-time authors being taken for a ride by the 'industry'. I escaped all such horrors with the inspirations by Mr. Sudhir Malhotra of Orient Paperbacks.

Last but not the least, there are numerous incidents and people who have been a part of this journey and I therefore dedicate each and every hour spent on creating this book to them.

But, most importantly, this is for you, my muse,...

- Akshat Jain

*"If thou must love me, let it be for naught
Except for Love's sake only"*

— ***Elizabeth Barrett Browning***

Contents

Prologue 1
Chapter Zero: Oh No! 7
Two Pearls in a Pod 17
Balancing Life 27
A Royal Debacle 37
180 Degree 45
Half-Acceptance 65
Don't Let Me Down 93
Deadlock 123
A Mistake to Be Proud Of 139
Life Equals Metamorphosis 157
Reflection 179
Epilogue 183

Prologue

Hey,

I wish I knew that things would turn out to be so difficult.

I know that this is the same clichéd line which every one of us keeps repeating throughout our lives. But I write this specifically for you.

I know that the phrase, 'I wish I knew,' works like a negotiator consoling my past, but it is really very difficult at this point of time to tell you the thing, or rather, things that are going on in my mind. It is hard to just suddenly jump to conclusions without filling in the big picture. So, I shall try my best. Yes, I know how love works here. I also know that the terms 'love' and 'marriage' cannot co-exist in this land without irrational hatred and a bit of internal fight. But love can exist, right? I mean, before and after marriage? Ok, I think now I am officially talking rubbish. Anyway!

Hey, you know, I think even getting an Austrian passport is easier than 'love-marriages' here. Yeah, feeling bored right? Or, aren't you?

You know, it is hard to tell something to you directly. Even when I am writing this letter, I am starting to think of the various things which you might be thinking of right now. It literally puts me in a state of paranoia to think that I am getting judged without even disclosing anything.

Couples around the globe marry when in love. But in some parts of the world, and especially in India, the term 'Marriage' is quite confusing. In India, 'Love' and

'Marriage' are thought to be two completely different entities. They can't exist together. If somehow they do, then the tedious process of bridging the gap between love and marriage is even harder than getting a US work visa or Austrian PR! However, love does exist in our land. Just before and after marriages. But only the latter is legal and accepted. Life is quite ironical tough. It takes sadness to know what happiness is, noise to appreciate silence, and absence to value the presence of someone very special. But the story I am going to tell you is quite different.

Once upon a time, there lived a Flamingo bird. But, why am I starting this paragraph with 'Once upon a time...'? Isn't that a stock phrase reserved for fairy tales or fantasy stories? Well, every story starts with a fairy tale and ends in reality. So, as the story goes, the Flamingo loved a Dove whose beauty was inexplicable. Her white feathers and beautiful beak crafted an indelible mark on the canvas of his mind. But there was a problem—the Dove lived in a land far away from the Flamingo and could not understand his love. But, as time rolled by, the Dove started developing feelings for the Flamingo and finally fell in love with him. The Flamingo, on the other hand, did not know that his sweet Dove was facing an internal strife about their future. Every day, they travelled large distances to catch a glimpse of each other. Love, as it is—the least understood thing in the world—caught hold of both of them. However, their tired wings never complained and even the sun hid itself behind the clouds when they both met each other. What an encounter it was! It seemed as if even nature sacrificed itself to bring both of them closer together.

Both of them started understanding each other and suddenly, one day, the Dove wanted to visit the Flamingo's nest. Hearing her request, he was overwhelmed and thus started making all sorts of preparations. He took care of each and every little thing which would otherwise cause discomfort to her. But when the Dove entered his nest, a sudden fear caught hold of her and all she wanted then was to leave that place. She wanted to come close to her Flamingo but was barred by that strange fear which bothered her from the very beginning. He tried his best to keep her comfortable in his cosy arms, but she flew away without a word. Shocked by such a sudden and unexplained departure, the Flamingo went to the Dove and asked her the reason for her discomfort. But the Dove could not explain her inner conflict and thus decided to split with him.

Heartbroken by her sudden decision, the Flamingo started hating himself and left his nest. Months passed by, but nobody saw him again in that area. He flew to different places and tried a lot to erase his feelings for the Dove. One evening, as the sun was about to touch the horizon, he felt thirsty and thus flew to a nearby pond to quench his thirst. The water was crystal clear and he could see in its reflection that his feathers had become rough and dull. Suddenly, he heard a low humming tune carried by the faint breeze. He followed the tune and was amazed to see a sunbird drinking water from the same pond. She looked at his dull and withered feathers and came over flying to give him a bit of company. After conversing for a minute or two, she asked him to take a dip in the pond along with her. Thus, in the quest for love, started another journey!

- Akshat Jain

Here we go...

Chapter Zero: Oh No!

"Who told you to ask her about her background and all?"

"What's up, man? It's 2:20 a.m. at night and you still fussing about that incident? Just get over it buddy. It was just a light interaction... That's all. Why are you going crazy over it?"

"Oh yes, Manav... I have a million reasons to go crazy right now. Do you even know that her uncle is in the CID[1]?"

"Ha-ha! What a joke! Her uncle, an actor? Which role in CID? These crazy people. Then why did her father send her here? She should be in some acting..."

"Bhai, I am talking about the real Criminal Investigation Department and not your Sony TV thing. He called me up and was enquiring about the entire matter."

"What? How did he get your number?"

"C-I-D, Manav. They don't find things. They extract their required info from the departments."

"Oh shit! And then what did you say about me?"

"Manav... I told him that you were our leader and that it was your plan to do all that."

"Gaddaaar nikla bhaaiii[2]... What did he say about me? Hey!! You, there? Hello... hey!"

It was nearly three o'clock at night and this sudden phone call from one of my classmates made me so agitated that I

---

[1] Criminal Investigation Department
[2] person who is disloyal or treacherous

was just restlessly waiting for the sun to rise. It was probably the longest wait of my life. The last time I ever waited for something this long was the India vs. Pakistan cricket match.

Look, everyone is brave until things go hay wire. And things had already turned into a complete mishap after this recent phone call. Well, let me tell you what the whole thing was: We were having some snacks in the corridor after out fourth lecture, and everything was pretty boring. My friends were asking me to sing a song so that they could finally laugh and have a bit of fun. The pressure from their side was very high, and I was just looking for some other distraction to bring amusement to my sweet batch-mates. At that very moment, I saw this girl coming up the stairs and immediately, I had this plan of interrogating her. I went like, "Guys! I have another plan. Gear up."

So yeah, she was Sweta, and was from the local area of Meerut[3] itself. The fun began when she fumbled to utter her father's name. It was really hilarious because she mistakenly told some weird surname of her father and we all laughed over it. She got so tensed and scared that she turned back and rushed down the stairs. And yeah, then I was the one who actually said, "Come-on! And these people think that they are going to crack interviews and get placed in companies. Hahaaa!"

The next day, just as I was about to step outside my house for the college, I got a call from an unknown number.

"Hello!"

"Hello, Mr. Manav, I am calling from the crime branch.

---

[3] City in the province of Uttar Pradesh

Please come over today at twelve. We want to have a talk with you."

And saying this, he hung up. I was stunnnnnned—totally from top to bottom! I knew that I was in some deep trouble now. I closed the door, turned around, and walked back into my home. But, seeing me entering, my mom bombarded me with thousands of questions. You know, mothers are the most caring as well as the most dangerous people on this planet. They can actually sense when something is wrong, and most importantly, they can sense it even when you do not utter even a single word.

But my mother's way of pressurizing me to open up about all the things was so intense that I said, "No maa, it's nothing with drugs and all. Please keep calm. I forgot to take my notebook. That's it." As I said this, she snatched my bag, opened it, and to my utter misfortune, found two beautifully covered notebooks inside. "So, now it is confirmed you are hiding something. Tell me what is it or I shall tell your dad," she threatened. Suspicion was at its heights, and I just somehow managed to run out of my house.

I had heard that CID men are quite punctual, and are extremely attentive to details. So I had taken care of everything. From my shoelaces to my hair, everything was neat and clean. It was 11:58 a.m. when I entered his office. He was a brown man with a thick moustache. He wore wide-framed spectacles and gave me a look which in itself implied that something very serious was about to happen.

"Sir, may I come in?" was my initial curtsey, but his reply was just a light nod. It was quite clear that I was about to get roasted and the grill was just being prepared. I went a step further, "Sir, may I have a seat?"

"No."

"Okhhay, sir. As you say." The 'No' was pretty stern. It was as if I had asked for his daughter's hand in marriage.

"So, Manav. You seem to have a lot of expertise in the sector of interviews."

"No sir, it was just like that. We were thinking of interacting with someone and Shweta arrived. It was all a coincidence, sir."

"Ohh! Coincidence, I see. Okhay... Let me take your interview then."

Yeah, this was the moment I had duly prepared for. I had read all the news headlines of the day and I had also done a prior research on all the criminal cases that the CID were currently handling. I was confident and said, "Yes sir, as you wish."

"So, Manav, how many stairs did you climb to reach my office?"

Look, this is why people say not to mess with these men. I was completely transfixed, and to make matters worse, he sprinkled a bit of salt on the wound saying, "Oh! And yes, let me help you a bit. We are in the second floor. The entire building is of three floors, and yes, there are no elevators in this building. You know, we also need to remain fit."

I was so badly stuck in the situation that all I could do was give him a weak smile and ask for forgiveness.

"No, Manav, you have to face the consequences. You

should have thought of all the consequences before doing whatever you did."

"I am sorry, sir. Very sorry! I shall do whatever you tell me to do but please forgive me."

I was badly sweating by then, and his horrific look made me even more tensed and terrified. He thought for some time and then said, "Ok. On one condition, I can let you free." This statement was a big relief for me.

"What sir? I am ready to do whatever you tell me to."

"Okhhay, so listen. One of my nephews, Kartik, is not listening to his father and wants to drop a year because he has not scored well in the entrance test. But his father and I want him to take admission in this university. Now, if you can talk to the administration about this and actually help him with the admission process, only then can I pardon you."

Okhay, now this was a real fit for me. I did have few good relations with the people in the administration, but I was highly unsure about whether I could actually carry this work out.

Well, as you can very well see, doing the work was the only option left for me. So, without thinking further, I promised to look into the matter.

Hearing a 'Yes' from me, he got up and said in a very satisfied tone, "Okhay then, come tomorrow to this address." I know that all this might sound a bit eerie, but yeah, it was at Kartik's residence that I landed the next day.

We shook hands. Kartik had long hair, and was kind of guarded in the way he talked. "So, what brings you here?" Well, the elaboration of the answer could have been a bit lengthy, so I thought of just sticking to two simple words—"Your Uncle!" Yes, Kartik was a bit perplexed when he heard this, but could not control his laughter once I told him the entire thing. However, the good thing was that Kartik was also interested in the Computer Science stream, which made my task a bit easier.

The next day, we went to our college admission office and there was this long queue of people standing to have a talk with the dean of admissions. It was a lengthy process consisting of a lot of visits and a lot of documentation. But, after a bit of persuasion, Kartik finally got in, and that too in the stream of his choice. This was a big relief, especially for me, and by this time, I think that CID sir was to a certain extent happy with me.

My eyes soon caught hold of this girl sitting down and writing something in the waiting area. Look, at this moment, some of you might think that I would go and try to talk to her. But, come on, this is our college and not a Bollywood movie! I did think of asking her about her stream and all, but I simply did not have that much courage left in me after what had happened a few days back.

I grew up in the city of Muzaffarnagar in the Sugar bowl of India—yes, Uttar Pradesh. My father had a business of sugar manufacturing, and we had a *haveli*[4] type house in which around 25 people lived. My routine during early childhood was simple—wake up at 6.30, put on the uniform, hop on to the school bus, sit in the class listening to irrelevant facts, look around at the pretty faces, reach home around three, do some

---

[4] A mansion is a very large house.

homework while desperately waiting for the clock to strike five, and once it strikes five, rush out with the cricket bat or badminton racquet. Or rush out to play 'I Spy' (also known as *Dhappa* in our playing terminology). After all that fun, rush back to home at seven or eight, gorge on the delicious dinner cooked by mumma, watch some television, get the bag ready for the next day as per the time-table, go to bed around 9.30 p.m., and then wake up again the next day at 6.30.

Only a few things in my routine managed to influence me: science, laws of science, and television shows like Captain Vyom.

I remember watching Doordarshan hindi news daily at 8 p.m. and English news like Agla Prasaran at 8.30 p.m. One had to watch them because there were no other better channels to switch to, and Doordarshan enjoyed the monopoly. In fact, such was its dominance that on weekends, the movie telecast would be halted for a hour just to show the news bulletins. Yups, one had to wait for an hour to watch the villain getting smashed in the climax. *Chitrahaar*[5] was also one of the shows that were close to my heart—a collection of seven-eight songs used to be telecast once a week at 7.30 p.m. in the evening, and every friend had to rush home to make sure they did not miss it. A few other shows like Rangoli, Mahabharat, Ramayan, and Chandrakanta[6] filled the Sunday morning with action.

Life was pretty easy and comfortable till I entered class X. After that, all the extraordinary relatives started showing their extraordinary care—"Child, this is an important year; you are now in tenth standard!" (Like I was not aware that I was in

---

[5] One hour TV program for songs
[6] Indian shows

tenth). Then they all quoted the same one-liner—*"is ek saal mehnat kar lo, jindagi ban jaegi"* (work hard this one year, and you will be settled for life). In one family function, I got the same kind of bulky words and heavy weight advice. But then, I was pretty much convinced that the board exams ought to be taken seriously. Finally, I cleared the board exams with good marks. It was supposed to be a rosy life filled with success after conquering Mount Class X. But, as you can see, I had been well deceived! Where is the palace, the wine, the jewels, the dancers? All the extraordinary relatives also went away, I don't know where.

My parents sensed that I was getting restless—the carrot was always diplomatically dangled just a couple of steps away. At the start of Class XII, I was told that the next two years were make-or-break and could shape my life. In the month of July, something unfortunate happened with me. I caught typhoid, and it stayed for the next 7-8 months. This was a shock for my family, and they even started doubting whether I would be able to take the board exams or not.

Finally, my efforts paid off, at least in terms of percentage scored, which was neither in the 90's nor the 80's. I just got 65.6 percent. I planned to drop one year to prepare for engineering entrance exams. Though it was considered fashionable at that time, I had a proper plan in my mind. After a year, I got a good rank in the engineering entrance exams. By then, people had started making an example out of me for their children and some of them started attaching the title of *'engineer sahib'*[7] to my name.

---

[7] Engineer Officer

Those days, computer science engineering seemed to offer better prospects, with the IT boom occupying maximum space in the conversations among middle class parents everywhere: charted buses, tea stalls near offices, and even morning walks.

So, I was all set to start a new journey with computer science engineering.

Two Pearls in a Pod

It was the second day of September in the year 2004, and I was in a hurry to attend my first class of college. I was running late, and was worried. People generally say that the first impression is the last impression, and that day, I was about to give my worst impression! All I had with me was a duffel bag, a lunch box, and a few notebooks. Entering the college, I went to a lecturer and asked, "Sir, where is the first semester's Computer Science class going on?" First, he gave me a slightly annoyed look and then said, "You are in the right floor, my boy. Now just go ahead and take a left, and then a right." I thanked him and rushed ahead. The campus had four buildings, out of which two were hostels, and the largest one was the engineering building. Our classes generally took place at the ground floor, and we also had a sufficiently large computer lab. There was also a library of 5000 square feet, and the rest of the campus consisted of buildings under construction and grassy fields.

So, here I was, rushing to attend my first class.

With every single step that I took towards my classroom, an uneasy feeling caught hold of me. I felt as if the board examination results had been announced once again, and that I was walking up to the notice board to check my results. What I felt then is quite inexplicable. It was just a mixture of many thoughts, which made me super excited. This happens with almost anyone who goes to college for the first time. The first day is always a bit different than the others. After all, new place, new level of education, and most importantly, new people. When I was a few steps away from the classroom door, I took a deep breath and then boldly went up and said, "May I come in, Ma'am?" Ms. Monika, the Maths lecturer, was taking the class. She got startled at my sudden approach and asked, "Who are you?"

"Ma'am, I am a fresher of the Computer Science branch."

"Oh, yes, please come in. Have a seat," she said.

I went inside, found one vacant seat, and took it. Everyone started staring at me as if I was either a celebrity or an odd duck amidst them. Ma'am was explaining our entire year's curriculum on the board, and I kept searching for a suitable spot in the lot.

After this started what I call 'the name-knowing' ceremony. I was in a way glad that the ceremony had not finished before my arrival and that I would get to know the names of these staring fellows. So she started with Neha, and at last came to me and asked, "So, what is your name?"

"Ma'am, my name is Manav."

"Oh Manav, please make sure you are not late to class, at least not to my class."

So, does she want to imply that I can be late to other lectures? Anyway, I just said, "Yes ma'am, I shall take care of that," and sat down.

I looked around and saw that the classroom was divided into two parts: one side for the boys and the other side for the girls. The first three rows seemed to be completely filled, and there were also some branch-mates sitting behind me. As I was looking around, my eyes caught hold of two girls who were sitting at the extreme corner of the third row bench. Out of the two, one looked like a tomboy. She had shaggy hair and a hoarse voice like that of a throat patient. Hearing her voice, it seemed like she had caught some throat infection. Her flawless caramel complexion and calm demeanour meant she was beautiful in an unconventional way, but she preferred to keep a low profile—attending classes and going home, paying no attention to the others unless absolutely necessary. Whatever the matter was, I remained busy examining the classroom, which seemed fairly charming to my eyes. I was especially fascinated with the walls and windows. The windows had glass panes which were coloured so that sunlight would not invade the comfort of our classroom, and the bars prevented further infiltration.

After a while, Ms. Monika asked me a few questions about my engineering entrance exam, native place, and the likes. The class got over in the next few minutes, and I thought of collecting some information about the class which I might have missed.

I was quite a shy guy, although not that shy either. But I had decided to maintain a proper decorum from the very beginning of the session. Everyone was talking to everybody else, and hence I decided to introduce myself to the ones sitting beside me.

I asked, "What all has happened since morning?"

"Well, nothing much. This was the first lecture on Maths-I. I don't know about the rest of the lectures," said the one sitting just beside me.

There were a few more lectures in the first half, and then there was the recess. During the recess, I went around the college gingerly with some of my classmates. There was always the fear of seniors like Rashmi Priya, which haunted us with every step we took inside the college campus. All of my batch-mates had this fear of being harassed, and thus, we preferred moving in groups. 'United we stand and divided we fall,' was the master plan for the time-being. However, most of us were residents of the local area, and thus we did not fear that much. Instead, we even thought of ragging some of our batch-mates. You know, just for fun—nothing that serious.

Our library was at the first floor just opposite to the staircase. I looked around the corner and slowly tiptoed my way inside the library. It was the quietest place in our whole campus, and I really liked spending my time in this big hall. Consequently, it was also the place where we did a lot of our mischief.

I went in and asked the Assistant Librarian, "Ma'am, what is the procedure to get books issued?"

"Are you a fresher?" she asked.

"Yes Ma'am."

"Alright, first you need to have the Library cards. I hope the cards will be issued to you within a few days."

This meant that I could not possibly borrow books before the cards were issued to us. Disappointed, I leafed though some books for a while and then left for the canteen. On my way to the canteen, I met one of the friends I had recently made, and he told me that after the break, a few lab sessions like Chemistry, Engineering Drawing, and Physics were scheduled. There is some sort of an inexplicable delight in figuring out a new place and getting to know the new people of that place. It makes you afraid at first, but at the same time, it expands your exposure to the world and introduces you to the new journey of life.

When I returned home after the hectic day, I decided to take a shower. After the shower, I went to the roof and sat there contemplating under the stars. Whenever I see stars, I often wonder how it all came into existence and who is behind its maintenance. It is as if there is some everlasting tune and harmony which binds us all together. A mystery unexplored, a note that keeps ringing but is never intercepted...

It was getting dark, and then came the call for dinner. After having my dinner, I looked into some of the courses and the upcoming assignments. There was this feeling of doing something interesting which kept knocking inside me. Yes, I am that kind of a guy who cannot live life without doing something mischievous.

The next day, I woke up early and entered the class exactly at the correct time. The previous day's experience had made me a little more punctual. However, this change was temporary, and was sure to be lost within a few months. The attendance of the class was low that day. It was just the start of the first week, and many new students were yet to be admitted.

It was a dull start, and thus I tried to mingle with one or two of my classmates. "Hey, how are you?" I asked one of them.

"Oh... Hi, you are Manav, right?"

"Yes, I am Manav. And you?"

"I am Ayush."

"Hi Ayush! You seem to be from the local area," I ventured.

"Yes, I am from Meerut itself. And you are from?"

"I am from M. Nagar."

"Oh... but where is it?"

"It is nearby."

Although he did not know the place, he still said, "Oh! Yes, M. Nagar. I got it."

Suddenly, another colleague replied, "I heard that nothing much is taught in the college classes.""

We both looked at his facial expression, and Ayush said, "Yes, you are right."

"Yes, I am seldom wrong my friend," he replied.

"Thank you. But who are you? I mean, what is your name?" I asked him.

"I am Vidyarthi."

"Hi!" I extended my hand towards him. "I think you know my name," I said.

"Of course. It's Manav, isn't it?" he said with a broad smile on his lips.

"Yes, it is. So, why such a low attendance today?"

"God knows! It might be because it is the second day. Generally, everyone appears on the first day, you know, just to know the place and get introduced to the courses," said Vidyarthi.

We three were sitting in the second row. And there was enough time left for the first lecture of the day to start. It was getting boring inside and thus we came out of the class in a group to enjoy the cool breeze in the corridor. Things were going real well until someone suggested me to sing a song. Yes, that incident happened after this.

As you know, it took me a few weeks to come out of that incident clean, and it also took me an additional four-five days to get back to my normal self. Yes, Kartik got admitted into our stream, but the problem was that he was behind in classes. So, I had to help him with notes and also had to brief him on whatever had been taught.

Then, one fine Monday, he came to class, and I immediately offered him a spot in our group. After all, I was grateful that the incident brought me a friend like Kartik.

After the first lecture was over, he said to me, "Let's take a round."

"But where?" I asked.

"Just nearby to the drinking area."

"Ok, let's go."

I closed my notebook and we went out.

So we walked till the canteen that was near our academic block. Although I used to visit the canteen in between classes, it was my first time there with Kartik. It was usual for Kartik to be a little intimidated. It was his first day in the college, and he made me promise that whatever happened, I should never leave him. I still remember how Kartik and I used to wait for the lectures to get over so that we could sneak out of the class and get a coffee between the lectures. Those days are still priceless for me.

One day after a few weeks, I was surprised to see one of my school mates walking inside the classroom, and I could not help but shout out loud, "Pankaj!"

He turned around in surprise, and broke out into a gleeful smile.

"Hey, Manav, you here?" he asked.

"Yes," I replied. "You have also taken admission here, right?" I asked.

"Yes, of course. I was surprised to see someone calling me by my name."

"Yeah. So, how is it that you are here?"

"My sister, Upasana and and I both took admission here. She is in the BCA academic block."

"Well, that's great! So, where are you sitting?"

"In the third-last bench."

"Hey, why don't you come over and sit here?"

"Yes, but I have got to do some work. I will catch up with you later."

"Alright bro, see ya."

Kartik and I were talking near a teashop when suddenly, he remarked, "There are very few girls in our class!"

I got mad at this statement and remarked, "Come on, bro! Please. It's good that there are not enough girls. Uff! If you would not have been admitted, I don't know what would have happened to me." Hearing this, Kartik burst into laughter and said, "Yeah! Alright, I apologize on my uncle's behalf. He is always a bit too harsh."

"Yes! That's true. But some more girls might join by the end of this month. So, have patience brother!"

And then we burst into laughter. We did not laugh at others, but at our own naughty thoughts. Kartik and I became fast friends, and we accompanied each other most of the time.

Every day after college, we used to sit in the tea-house outside the college campus and discuss various topics. We loved the tea there, and it served as a refreshing drink for our exhausted minds. Fuelled by the energy of antioxidants, we used to indulge ourselves in mischievous activities. They were not actually naughty, but gave us great fun. My dear friend, Kartik, was an ambivert, and was intelligent as well. He used to play safe tricks intelligently. But I used to go bold and risked myself at almost any random activity. Growing along the same paths of the daily academic routine, life had taken a new turn. There was now a new opportunity, a new way.

Balancing Life

It was my first year in the college, and things were going pretty well. I had made some great friends and took my studies very seriously. Albert Einstein once said that for keeping the balance while riding a bicycle, we must pedal forward. And that was exactly what I was doing in my day-to-day life. Things had begun to take a new turn, and I met with some wonderful teachers with whom I made everlasting relations. I had been good at Physics and Mathematics since my engineering entrance exams preparation days, and thus always craved to answer most of the questions asked by our lecturers. I can never forget Alok Garg sir. He used to take our Physics and Mathematics classes, which I enjoyed a lot. His method of teaching was quite organic, and he always used to explain everything in a practical way. I was also very much fond of subjects related to electrical engineering, which were mostly taught by Yatish Chaturvedi sir. He was a young guy and always used to crack jokes in our class. I loved him a lot, and I had never seen a jollier man in my life. He used satire to teach the necessary lessons of life. I remember one of his classes in which he explained to us how we often misjudge things in life. His words were something like this:

"I know that you all are feeling bored and want to go to sleep. But, there is something important which I want to tell you. See, once it happened that a black woollen cloth was seen floating along the river Ganga. There was a full-scale row over that floating blanket. The air was flooded with various types of opinions from the intelligent people of the society. They said that it was a very precious blanket that had been sent to earth by Lord Shiva. Some grown-up people said that it contained some message from the almighty. Well, the Ganga in those days was very clean, and thus the woollen blanket could not be excused for an old rag from the cold storages or the jute factories. But in the midst of all this commotion, there stood a man who was nearly in his thirties. Seeing the black blanket going up and down with the waves, he wondered what would happen if he could take that piece of cloth with him. He heard his fellows say that it contained some hidden message from heaven. All these provocative thoughts made him go crazy and he finally jumped into the river to get hold of the blanket. As he approached the blanket, he felt claws grasping his legs. It was a bear and not a blanket! The high waves made it look like a blanket."

We all laughed to our heart's content at the foolishness of that man. But the stark reality is that we all become that man once in our lifetime. No matter what, we get lured and deviated from the reality and jump ashore to get hold of the illusion. We keep running forward to reach the mirage of happiness. Sorry for being so dramatic, but this is the most inevitable truth of life.

Out of all those who studied with me, I was the one with the highest rank in the engineering entrance exams. It was a matter of pride for me and I considered myself to be studious. Well, to put it straight, I was not that studious either. I never could sit in one place with my books for more than three hours. But for those three hours, I was the most serious person in the world, and sat in the same place like the statue of my grandfather cut out of stone.

Every day, when we entered the college in the morning, we were handed that day's newspaper. Don't worry, we had to pay for that—nothing was ever for free! The newspaper was provided to us for keeping pace with the ever-changing world and its ways. But as you can well comprehend, we were not at all interested in the world and its political ways. We had our own world, our own ways, and our own problems. So, we used those newspapers to make paper boats in the monsoon and aeroplanes during the summer. We often tore papers intentionally and littered our classroom. The newspapers remind me of Mr. Rathi. One day, he started a fire with a bundle of papers and started chanting hymns. He called himself the *"pandit*[8]*"*. He was completely out of his mind, and we had to pour water from our bottles to put out the fire. The whole classroom was filled with smoke, and we were all scolded terribly by the Deputy Director. The smoky smell stayed for days, and Rathi was not seen in the classroom for weeks. People also used to set off firebombs with timers using incense sticks or the sticks of Good night mosquito coils.

Talking so much about crackers reminds me of the lights, colours, sweets, greetings, blessings, family, friends, and fun as well. Yes, it was Diwali, the festival of lights. It is one of the most awaited festivals in our annual calendar. The sparks and lights and emotions make it a perfect amalgam of fun and enjoyment. Firecrackers are sold ten days prior to the festival. The pavements and market squares get filled with firecrackers of different types: sparklers, rockets, whistle bombs, and many more. Candles and glass bangles are also sold. There is fun and merriment all around.

---

[8] A Brahmin scholar or a teacher of any field of knowledge in Hinduism, particularly the Vedic scriptures, dharma, Hindu philosophy, or secular subjects such as music. He may be a Guru in a Gurukul

I can clearly remember that day when Kartik brought some fire-crackers to the classroom. It was great fun bursting one of those between the lectures. Terror spread all over the canteen and the boys' washroom. We even lighted a firecracker in the library. What a reaction that got from those avid readers! Our librarian had gone for a cup of tea, and we seized this opportunity to scare those who were inside the library. We lighted the whistling bomb with a small incense stick and placed it inside one corner of the library. It was like a time bomb. After four minutes, it went off, and everyone was taken aback. They were shocked as if the whole world has broken loose on them. It was great fun that day.

On the day of Diwali, we would break all protocols and ride our bikes all over the city. We would bring sweets for our neighbours and wish everyone on social media. As you can see, we could not afford those costly missiles that fly up and explode. So we used to watch others' crackers burst and brighten the sky. Sudden explosions could be heard in each and every corner of the city.

Well, I studied a lot in the first year of engineering and burnt the midnight oil so that I could do well in the terminal exams. I studied whenever I got time in the classroom, library, or even in the canteen. I had started solving problems on Schrodinger's equation—one of the toughest topics of physics in engineering. Besides studies, I did not have much to do. After our exams got over, we were eagerly waiting for our results. Every day, we could hear rumours like "the results are going to be declared tomorrow," "the results are out and many people have failed," and so on.

Finally, after a couple of weeks, the results were released at midnight. The irony of the situation was that I was unaware of the fact that the results were out. It was a sunny, winter morning of December, and I walked inside the college, stood in front of *Maa Saraswati's* (Goddess of education in India) statue, and folded my hands. This statue was placed just at the front basement of the entry gate, and it was the place where everyone prayed for her blessings.

Out of the blue, I heard a voice from behind.

"Hi, Manav."

I turned back and found that it was Mansi.

She was not aware that I didn't even know about the results being declared.

"My results are very bad, Manav. I got a back in two subjects in the first year itself!"

"What? Results are out?"

"Yes, they came out last night."

"Oh God! Who topped?"

"You."

"What! Really?"

"Yes, you have topped. Go and see the notice board."

After hearing this, I was overjoyed and all that went through my mind was a feeling of deep satisfaction. My hard work had finally given me fruitful results. I rushed towards the classroom. Kartik, Vikrant, and Ayush were standing near the podium with the Mathematics lecturer ma'am, Anupama. I shouted, "Results are out!" All of them stared at me.

"Yes, we were about to tell you, but we did not have your number," said Kartik.

Vikrant came and hugged me tightly, and Anupama ma'am congratulated me. She said, "But I am not happy with your results, Manav. You have got only 81% in Mathematics. I expected more from you. Maths paper was easy this time."

Mansi came up and said, "Congratulations, Manav."

"Mansi, how were your results?" I asked.

"It's fine. But not like yours! Great performance, huh?" Mansi replied.

"Thanks," I replied.

There were a few other students as well, and all of them congratulated me. I went down to the ground floor, called up my parents, and informed them about my results. I then went up and headed towards the canteen.

"Hey buddy, let's have a party," said Kartik.

Other guys from the hostel and other branches were also present there.

Vikrant said, "Hey, at least give us a small cold drink party. We will have the bigger party afterwards. You are the topper of four branches out of the five branches. Come on!"

I conceded to their request and told our canteen boy to hand over soft drinks to all my friends who were present there. Anupriya from the Information Technology branch was also standing there. Kartik indicated to me to offer her a drink too. I handed over a drink to her and she congratulated me.

Kartik and I used to meander here and there throughout the campus quite often. After every lecture, it was our habit to take a brisk walk along the corridor. Although it was not mandatory, we needed a bit of refreshment after those long, tiresome lectures. As I told you before, we were good friends, the best of all. That day, one of our friends, Deepak Yadav, could not be seen anywhere. We figured that he might be in the hostel, and went there to meet him. When we reached, we found that his room was shut from the inside and there was complete silence. We knocked on the door, and then, after few minutes, Deepak opened the door. He was crying, and from his face, we could make out that it was definitely something regarding the exams. After conversing with him, we came to know that he had failed in three subjects and that too in the first term itself.

It was heartrending for all of us. We looked at each other and then consoled Deepak. He was sobbing and we could not bear that. After all, he was one of our best friends.

"Hey Deepak, it's not a great deal, buddy. You can make it up in the second term," said Kartik. "Hey, it's not the end of the world. Come on! Let's take a walk."

I held his hand, pulled him up, and told him, "We all are there with you, Deepu. Come on! All will be ok."

Little did we know that we were talking to the future Air Force Officer of India! We walked down the stairs and out to the field. We talked our hearts out for hours and had a few cups of tea together. Deepak got cheered up and we all felt happy. When the sun was about to touch the horizon, we decided to head back home. One by one, everyone started to leave. When everybody had left, I went to the class, took my bag, and headed home.

Through the entire first year, my life went from 'good' to 'worse,' and then lifted itself to 'better.' There were some good professors, but they were hugely outweighed by the others who were not that good. I know that I should not start a comparison here, but yes, I can't help it this time. We could see from our windows cattle and peacocks roaming inside the campus. Since it was September, the weather was hot in north India. It was a tough task to reach college every day, and getting back home was tougher because of the forty-degree heat during daytime.

By the end of our second year, I learned all possible techniques to make the cut possible. I was already preparing smalls slips, normally referred to as *'farre'*[9], and was arranging books which could be hidden in college washrooms for aiding us with our exams. Throughout the first year, many students, including me, passed our exams only with the help of such crafty weapons. During the exam, we would visit the washroom, refer to the book, and go back to the class to write the answer.

By this time, I had made one good friend called Raju. He was an admin staff and photostat machine operator. I offered him some flexi benefits and convinced him to help me. When I was having tea and snacks at the canteen a couple of days before the exams, he told me that professors had got to know that students were keeping books in the

---

[9] Hand written notes used to cheat in exams.

washrooms just before the exams, but he assured me that he would be around to help me out. This was a relief indeed. You see, that's the kind of person whom we call a friend—someone who is there for you in times of need.

However, just before the first exam, one of the professors came and announced that they had sanitized the washrooms. This dropped like a bomb on the class. I saw many faces turning pale. But I had full faith in Raju. I looked out of the window, and there he was standing. He looked at me, gave me a thumbs up and pointed at his wristwatch to indicate that the game was on. That was the day I got a tremendous amount of self-confidence and started believing that I was indeed a genius.

A Royal Debacle

It's all happening so fast, isn't it? It has just been a few pages and we are already in the third year of college. I can clearly remember that it was winter, and severe cold winds were blowing rampant all over the city. To escape its clutches, we were all sitting inside a coffee shop and planning for Neha's (Mansi's only and best friend) birthday party, which was the next day. We all were busy gossiping about the decoration, balloons and other stuff, and were taking a sip of the warm coffee every now and then. When we were done with our planning and other talks, we departed.

That night, we were all waiting for the clock to strike twelve so that we could flood her timeline with wishes. The anticipation and long wait was a source of great fun, and the next day, we all gathered at the canteen. A cake was arranged and some candles were bought from the nearby store. She cut the cake and we all wished her a happy birthday. Everyone was enjoying themselves that day. We were singing randomly, and there were no boundaries that could hold us back. After a while, everyone thought of playing a game. So we all gathered around the table and were gossiping, punctuating chatter with giggles and laughter. The game was pretty simple—the intention was to find out the names of everyone's crushes. Not everyone had feelings for someone, but there were a few of us who were into relationships, and they did admit that without any hesitation. The unusual stares and tensed laughter went on for a while. Everyone blabbered out their secrets one by one, and after Pankaj, it was the turn of Mansi. She suddenly got on her feet and with a tone of disdain said, "No, I don't like anyone in the college."

"Oh really, Mansi...," went some of the boys sitting on the opposite side.

Suddenly, Neha gave Karan a wink to indicate that there was actually someone among the lot for whom Mansi had feelings. Karan caught that straight, and without any further delay, cleared his throat and added fuel to the fire saying, "So how about Vikrant, or Pankaj, or Manav, or, or what about Kartik?" As soon as he took the name of Kartik, I saw Neha gently pressing the left foot of Karan, and everyone was sure that it was Kartik. Out of utter embarrassment, Mansi left the place immediately, and Neha followed her. Kartik and I could not figure out the matter and remained flabbergasted while the others kept giggling and making silly remarks. The day ended in complete chaos, and Kartik left after that incident. I never took the matter seriously, but what happened that day spread like wildfire throughout the college. Within a few weeks, it became the topic of discussion for everyone. It was especially embarrassing for Kartik. He started skipping classes, and I could understand his problem. Not that I had faced such a situation before, but one can always understand someone's frustration under such circumstances.

So, the whole matter continued for a prolonged time, and I really wanted to help my friend who was in dire straits. I clearly remember that it was a resplendent Sunday morning, and I was sitting on a couch, reading the newspaper and sipping warm coffee every now and then. Out of the blue, my phone rang, and it was Kartik. I sat up straight, and sliding to accept the call, said in a broken tone, "Hi Kartik, how are you?"

"Jain, please come to my room at around 3:00 p.m. this afternoon."

"Hey, is there some sort of a problem?"

"Nothing much, just wanted to close this matter once and for all."

I was taken aback for a moment, but eventually said, "Alright, I will be there. Don't worry."

I set off at noon and reached his room at around 2:30 p.m. When I reached there, I found him soundly asleep. This was extremely frustrating—I wait the entire moment to hear what the problem was, and when it is finally time, I find him sleeping. Anyway, I shook him awake and Kartik asked me to have a seat.

"Ok! Ok! But what has happened?"

"Yaar, I think this matter has gone quite viral all over the campus, and so I have decided to put an end to it."

"Ok, so what have you thought regarding this? I mean, how are you going to close this thing?"

"Yaar, I have called Mansi today to Sai Restaurant. We will meet and clarify all doubts."

I started feeling a bit weird. I did not know what was going on, and had no idea about what was going to happen. I was having that sort of ill feeling that you get when you are in an internal controversy about your answer being correct in the examination hall when it does not match with anyone else's.

"So, am I to go there too?"

"Yes Manav, for sure. You are, after all, my best friend."

You see, I was indeed his best friend, and I had no other option than to go with him. Kartik looked troubled, and I could not afford to not go with him under such circumstances. After all, 'A friend in need is a friend indeed.'

So we walked all the way to Sai Restaurant [10] and found Mansi and Neha waiting there for us. This was the first time my eyes caught hold of Mansi, and I will not deny that for the first time in my life, I felt that little pinch of infatuation in my heart. This might sound very immature, but I could not help but notice her orange scarf. I had never seen her in that kind of an attire before. It was neither modern, nor too old-fashioned. It could be simply defined as 'classic.' They were shocked to see me, which made me feel like an unwanted intruder. However, we went inside and took our seats. I could see that Kartik was feeling a bit uncomfortable, and hence I broke the ice by saying, "Alright then. You guys have your conversation. Neha and I will wait outside." Neha agreed to that and we came outside. I had been curious from the very beginning, and out of anxiety as well as excitement, I asked Neha, "So what is that Mansi wants to talk?"

She gave me a blank look and bluntly replied, "I don't know."

I could understand that she knew everything but didn't want to reveal anything to me. I took another glance at the glass pane to catch a glimpse of Mansi but could not see her. There was quite a crowd inside, and my conscience also held me back from peeking too hard. It was like finding two pieces of wheat-grain in two bushels of husk. It felt simply

---

[10] Restaurant in the name of God "Sai"

dumb to stand outside the restaurant with an unknown girl so that my friend could talk to his so-called girlfriend and fix things up. It had been more than thirty minutes, and I was starting to lose my patience. I rang Kartik up and he said that he needed more time. By now, it was starting to get unbearable, and I could not help but tell him that I could not wait any longer. Kartik seemed pretty cool and said, "Alright bro, go home. Thanks for coming. I shall talk to you tomorrow." This was simply, WOW. I come with my friend and then go home after standing outside a restaurant for more than thirty minutes. Yes, you can consider this as one of the side-effects of having a 'best friend' like Kartik.

On my way home, I started having absurd thoughts: Kartik and Mansi, the two stars of our college. They are good at English, Aptitude, and many other things. They are sure to make a good couple. May be it would be a good choice. But what I came to know the next day was completely the opposite. Whether it was due to some weird fascination or some uncertain thoughts of Kartik or because of his dominating nature, I don't know, but Kartik had developed a feeling of strong repulsion towards Mansi. However, I started to convince Kartik regarding Mansi.

I was really sad to see Kartik in such a state. So, one day, I decided to take Kartik to the Gol Market[11] in Meerut Cantonment area. It was a very calm and quiet place filled with greenery and chirping birds. There was also a zoo nearby, and I made sure to visit that place at least twice a month. We were sitting on the brick wall adjacent to the zoo area near the Gol market and were having a cup of coffee.

---

[11] Local market built in the form of a semicircle

Minutes flew past in silence, and it seemed as if Kartik was feeling annoyed. I could no longer tolerate this silence and said, "Kartik, you know one thing?"

"No, I don't. Please tell me."

"Yaar, Mansi is a good girl. Just accept her proposal."

"Nah, I never thought or even considered her as anything more than a friend, and now I come to know this."

"Know what yaar? That she loves you, right? So what's the problem in that?" I asked.

"You won't understand it anyway."

"Yes, obviously I won't understand because you never tried to make me understand."

"I don't know. Seriously Manav, I don't have that type of feeling for her."

"But she loves you Kartik," I said.

"Yes, I know that but..."

"Come on buddy, she loves you, and she is a very good girl. At least think about her feelings and emotions."

"Alright Manav, if she is that good and you care so much about her, then why don't you go and ask her out, huh?"

"Kartik, that's not the point. The thing is that she loves you and she really cares about you."

Suddenly Kartik said, "Don't give me lectures!" and went off with the empty glass in his hand. I saw him walking away in rage and decided to remain silent.

I could not figure out the reason for his anger. I could neither understand his problem with Mansi nor fathom his inner frustration. I decided to give him some space and thus did not contact him for a few days. He started skipping classes and I became worried. After all, he was my good friend, and I could never give up on him. Days passed in utter frustration, and then, suddenly one day, around the time winter was on the verge of ending, Kartik showed up. He was running a high fever, but seemed to ignore me. He had changed quite a lot, much beyond my imagination. He stopped sitting with me in class and never went out after the lectures. I used to wait for him in the canteen with anticipation, but he never came. I was annoyed and thus diverted my attention away from him and left him to his fate. It was heartrending to see such a great friend ignoring me for no certain cause. Our friendship, which had been the strongest, turned out to be fragile when put to test! I don't know, maybe this is what happens when you try to do a good turn to some people—they push you away.

180 Degree

I was certainly busy with my life, but those words of Kartik did hurt me deeply. I was just trying to help him out, but on the other hand, he taunted me to go and propose to Mansi. This was really awkward, and thus I thought it would be right to inform Mansi about this situation. Although I was ready to go and start the conversation, there was that same fear which crept inside my heart and barred me from making any sort of uncalculated progress. However, after a week of endless thinking, I went ahead and talked to her. Soon, Mansi and I became quite good friends and talked almost every day. Our topics of discussion mostly included our ambitions, studies, placements, and the like. But her curiosity lay only with one person, and that was Kartik. She always inquired about him, and asked me whether he had said anything to me about her.

The only problem was time. Although we managed to meet for a few minutes during the recess, it was never sufficient. Thus, I decided to ping Mansi on Gtalk window.

"Hi Mansi!"

"Hi! Who are you?"

"U know me very well. Not very well maybe, but yes you know me."

"Oh…Manav? Wow! Suddenly here on Gtalk?"

"It's not suddenly, Mansi. I have been on Gtalk since class 11th!"

"Hmn."

"So, how are you?"

"I'm fine. What about you?"

"Yeah, Mansi. Just trying to be fine. You know, a lot of studies."

"Yeah. Seriously! Sometimes I get headaches, Manav. I feel this academic routine is going to be hard to pull through."

"Ha-ha! That's true. The syllabus is really huge," I typed.

"Have you heard the lectures? I go to sleep every time. They are so boring."

"Yeah. I like the lectures though. They are not that great, but they are good."

"Oh yes! I forgot that I was talking to the branch topper."

This was clear flattery. But anyway, I typed, "No, it's nothing like that."

"Hmn."

Her 'Hmn' thing really turned me off.

"See Mansi, I know that you have feelings for Kartik, and I seriously can't understand his problem."

"..."

Seeing her typing something and then deleting it, I was quite annoyed. After all, I wanted to be friends with her and the first thing in friendship is trust. So I typed, "Oye, write it. Don't stop. I know how you are feeling."

"Who told you that I have feelings for Kartik?"

"Mansi, I guess the whole college knows about it."

"…"

"Come on, Mansi. Just admit it."

"It's not that easy, ok! Yes."

"Ok…Ok…Calm down, madam."

"He hurt me a lot. Do you know what happened that day in the restaurant?"

"Well, I don't."

"Very good… No need to know."

"It's alright, Mansi. Just calm down; he has behaved rudely with me as well."

"Yeah whatever…"

"So Mansi, tell me a bit about yourself. I mean, only if you want to."

"I am feeling very sleepy today."

"Oh! I am so sorry. Good night then."

"Yes. Good night."

"Good night Mansi."

"Hmn. Good night."

"See you tomorrow at the campus ma'am."

"I don't know whether I will go tomorrow or not."

"Alright, if you come, then we shall meet. I mean, if you want to."

"Yes sure. And yes sir, no need to be so formal."

"Ha-ha. Ok! Good night then."

"Yes. Good night."

The next day, I went inside the classroom and was eagerly waiting for her. The most serious outcome of the whole chain of incidents was that I started having feelings for Mansi. I did not like Kartik's behaviour towards her, and even this thing bugged me day and night. So, had I started developing feelings for Mansi? Well, it is quite difficult to say actually. I think that I had developed some sort of care for Mansi by this time. But all that I ever wanted was to solve the problems between Mansi and my friend. Kartik was one of my very close friends, and I did not want to see him in such emotional turmoil. It might look like I am trying to suppress and hide things within me, but actually, all this was happening for the first time. Yes, first time, at least for me. Then came Kartik with his gloomy face. He went straight to the back, without even looking at me. This was what bothered me. Here I was, always wishing well for my friend, and on the other hand, he did not even care. Yes, he did not know that I was trying to settle things between him and Mansi, but at least he could have talked to me. His utter indifference towards me was just not acceptable to me. There were times when I went ahead to communicate with him, but he kept ignoring me every single time.

I returned home, and without even changing my clothes, grabbed my phone and started checking the chats for any update. But there was not even a single message from her. Thus, I decided to wait a little longer and went to take a shower. After getting refreshed, I finally sent her a message:

"Hey. How are you?"

She did not reply for a long time, and so I went for a nap. When I woke up, I found three messages:

"Hey!"

"I am fine."

"So sir, how was college?"

I was a little excited to see her messages and quickly replied,

"Yeah, it wasn't that good, but it was okay."

And then I sat waiting, waiting, and waiting for her reply. After fifteen minutes came her reply:

"Well! So, Kartik went today?"

"Yes! He went. He always behaves as if we are complete strangers. I think I should stop bothering about what he thinks and does."

"Hmn."

"What hmn?"

"No. Actually, your friend has changed a lot. That is the thing. I never expected to find him like this."

"So, you know him from a long time before?"

"Nah nah! The first time he came for the admission, I was sitting there filling up my admittance form. That is when I saw him."

"So, for you it was a love-at-first-sight thing?"

"Yeah, you can say so. We even talked for a few days. But now he has completely changed."

"Okhay. But he never told me anything about you. Anyway, I told him a lot about you and your feelings and that you really love him."

"Who said that I love him?"

"Oh come on, Mansi, please... So, now you are implying that you don't love him?"

"Hmn... I had feelings for him but I don't love him. Love takes time, and after all, he turned out to be a creep."

"Ha-ha. That's true, even I never expected him to become like this."

"He has some sort of problem I think. He behaves in such an absurd way nowadays. Now I think that all you boys are the same."

"Hmn, may be!"

"What hmn?"

"Nothing ma'am, Hmn means Hmn."

"Hmn then..."

"Hmn... Hmn..."

"Ha-ha. Stop it now Mr."

"Sorry!"

"No need to say sorry Mr."

"Hmn"

"Well, so how are you Mr.?"

"Not well. Actually I'm feeling a bit off. Things were going perfect just a few days ago."

"Yes, it happens sometimes. I know."

"Do u know something?"

"What Mr.?"

"I like talking to you."

"Oh...really?"

"Yes ma'am."

"Well, I like talking to you as well. At least you are not creepy like the other guys. Or should I say, 'Maybe.'"

"Ha-Ha, yes you are rather implying 'maybe.' But you know that there are always exceptions to things in nature."

"Yeah, exceptions! Maybe"

"Hey, do you still feel for Kartik?"

"I don't know. I don't think I do. After all, a girl's heart is an ocean of secrets."

"Seriously? What secrets?"

"It's nothing. I was just joking. Haven't you watched Titanic?"

"Ohh! Yes, yes. I have watched that movie. It is just awesome. Every time I watch it, I feel that I am watching it for the first time."

"Yes, I love that movie too. The love story is so intense. I wish I were Rose and then I would meet Jack!"

"Yes, I wish I were Jack. I really loved his artistic skills."

"Which scenes do you like the most?"

"Well, there are many. But, there is one scene where Jack dies and Rose sings 'Come Josephine in my Flying Machine.' That part really makes me emotional."

"Yes, Sir. But I don't like the ending. There was plenty of space for Jack to hold onto. But he intentionally did not."

"Ha-ha. Maybe!"

"Maybe? What 'Maybe'? Of course there was space for Jack. There was a lot of space for Jack."

"Okhhay... Okhhay...Hey, are you coming tomorrow?"

"Yes. You?"

"Yuup girl, I am going. I seldom miss classes."

"Yes, yes. Mr. Topper!"

"Ha-ha!"

"So, you studying now?"

"No. I am just lying on my bed."

"Good. I am lying on my bed too."

"Good. Take some rest, madam."

"I have been taking rest from the very morning itself, sir."

"Oh! What did you do from morning?"

"Well, I did some work—cleaned some utensils, and then I studied a bit and later went to the garden to water the plants."

"Wao. You can cook? I did not know that."

"Yes. I am a very good cook. Like my mom."

"Someday I wish to eat food cooked by you."

"Ha-ha. Yes. Sure."

"It's quite good to hear that you manage to do so many things by yourself. I am completely useless. I never help my mom. Well, I sometimes do the monthly shopping and bring her medicines."

"Hey. I am facing a problem in the Maths project. I am quite confused."

"Don't worry Miss, I will give you my project and then you can see that and clarify all your doubts."

"Thank you so much professorJ."

"You are most welcome."

"Is there something I can do for you, sir?"

"Yes. But I don't know whether you would like that or not."

"Come on. Don't be shy with me. Just say it to me."

"Alright, alright. If I need to discuss something, can we talk over the phone?"

"..."

"... ..."

"Alright madam, I got it. No need to talk."

"When did I say that I don't want to talk? Don't make assumptions so fast."

"So give me your number miss."

"Check your Contacts section."

"Got it. I am calling you now."

"Ok. Call me."

During our chats, she often mentioned ways to convince Kartik and always wanted to know his impact on such operations. But as time rolled on, Kartik's topic slowly evaporated from our daily conversations and we started talking to each other regarding our families and our customs and just things related to us two only.

We talked for nearly an hour, and then while I kept talking, suddenly the notification bell rang and there was this message from Mansi:

"Hey, what just happened?"

"Nothing. My phone's balance is low and the call got disconnected suddenly."

"Don't worry, professor! I will recharge your phone tomorrow."

"There is absolutely no need for doing that Miss."

"You have a husky voice."

"Ha-ha! Your voice is rather sweet."

"Oh really, mister?"

"Yes. Really!"

I knew she was smiling on the other end and I was smiling too. We started chatting for hours until it was 3:00 a.m. Each and every conversation with her was my favourite one. When it got very late, we used to stop the conversation and preserve some talks for the next day. This was our ideal explanation for ending the conversation. And I still remember that night. I was so excited that I could not manage to fall asleep. May be because I was waiting for the clock to strike 9:30 so that I could go to college, or may be because I again wanted to call her up and talk to her. Those days, college had become very interesting for me. I did not take leave even for a single day, and wanted to attend every single day of the college. The days were passing by very fast and my only intention was to enjoy as much as I could in the remaining college time. It became one of our customs to take photographs of every event that took place on the campus. After all, these were memories only to be kept safe within.

A few days later, Neha came up to me with a face filled with mirth and peculiar expressions and went, "Manavvvv!"

"Hey!" I replied.

"You know Manav, Mansi waits for your phone call and stays awake till late at night. She clings onto the phone so that she might take your call within two or three rings itself."

"Oh, hello girl! Come on..."

"Ohhh! Our boy got some attitude, I see..."

This is what I call as the teasing factor. I was feeling a bit embarrassed and thus left the place. Two of my friends burst out into laughter and started giggling. I was feeling happy within, but I was not sure whether she felt the same for me or not. Moreover, I did not have the courage to ask her out at that very moment and wanted time to play its part. You know, it is human nature to be a little restrained before delving into something serious and irreparable, and hence it was tough for me to hurry up.

Everything was going fine for the next few weeks. Mansi and I used to talk almost everyday and on one such day, I asked her about her zodiac details. I do not know why I did that; maybe that I was curious to know what the stars said about us.

She said, "What will you do with my zodiac details?"

"Nothing, will you please give me your details? Please," I replied.

I think she understood why I was so eager to know about her zodiac details and so, without further ado, she volunteered it.

I had the landline phone just beside me, and I immediately called up Kartik and said, "Hi, how are you?"

"Why? So ardent today, I see. What was the ill fate that required you to contact me, huh?" he said.

"Well, can you please tell me your zodiac details?"

"Why?"

"No, I mean, just like that. I wanted to check some career-related predictions. Will you please tell me? Trust me."

He agreed to it and told me his details as well. I got over-excited and opened the horoscope software in a hurry. I turned to the compatibility page and entered Kartik's and Mansi's zodiac details. I told her that there were some things which matched between Kartik and her. I don't know what her actual reaction was, but she chuckled and, with a tone of utter disdain, replied, "Hmn."

I was curious about how my stars aligned with hers, and thus I typed in my details in place of Kartik's. But I found out that none of the important things matched between us. I had the phone in one hand and suddenly, I came back to my senses and heard Mansi saying over the phone, "Hey, what happened? Why are you so silent?"

I was lost for words and said to her, "Nothing. I was just checking something."

"What were you checking?" she asked.

"It's nothing," I said, "I am feeling sleepy today. Good night Mansi."

"Hey, what happened so suddenly?" she asked.

"Nothing, I just dozed off. Good night."

"All right, Good night. Take care."

I was in utter disbelief. I re-entered my details, but the results were the same. Although I did not blindly believe in astrology, I was still a bit upset with the results. After gazing at the screen for sometime, I fell asleep.

The next morning, I was quite refreshed. I thought to myself that astrology could not always be right, and after all, love overpowers all sorts of predictions. It was something of a 'grapes are sour' type of conclusion. But when something goes against your wishes or your expectations, you generally have a tendency to be in denial and find faults with the results. I don't know why it is so, but it gives us a hope of doing something from scratch once again. I had always been trying to convince Kartik to accept Mansi's proposal and respect her feelings, but somewhere down the line, in my endeavour to bring both of them together, I had started developing irresistible feelings for Mansi.

The days of college were coming to an end, and everyone was getting more and more worried about their own future. No one could be seen fooling around anymore, and suddenly, everyone had started taking time seriously. The library seldom remained empty, and most of the important books went missing. All were down to the rat race! I was rather steady with my studies and so I did not have to rush like the other people at the last moment. I had all my notes with me, and I was quite well prepared with the lessons. But the main problem was finding a job. Everyone had their own opinions about the difficulties of finding a job. But I never felt that much tensed because, in the meantime, I found out that proposing to the love of your life is much more challenging than finding a job of your choice. Sometimes, I would dream of taking birth in a planet where a day would consist of 48 hours, because I felt as if the 24 hours on this planet were generally shrinking. I was confused about whether life was becoming faster or the days were becoming shorter and shorter. But I did not have time to clarify that confusion as well. People say that we are fighting with nature, and some say that we are fighting with ourselves. But I say that we are constantly fighting with time, because it is the single aspect of nature that drags you to your grave, and you literally have to keep running at a steady pace to stay on board.

So, in the last year of engineering, we had the opportunity of seeing many companies visiting our campus to offer lucrative jobs to us. Well, the jobs were not that lucrative either! And the ones who bagged them were quite small in number. We had to burn the midnight oil in preparation, and the most challenging part was the interview. One day, Wipro Limited came to our college. Their selection process was held in three steps: written examinations, followed by the communication round, and lastly the interview. The first day was generally reserved only for female candidates, and the day after was for us.

There was commotion from the very morning itself. I saw Mansi getting ready for the examination. I went up to her and said, "All the best! It will all turn out to be fine." And then I smiled a bit. Her face was filled with anxiety and tension which, under those circumstances, was normal. Hearing my words, she smiled a bit and said, "Same to you for tomorrow. Hope it all goes well. Bye!" And then off she went along with the flock. I don't know why but yes, by heart, I wanted her to get the job. I wanted things to be better for her. I was well aware that she had faced rejection from the very onset of her life, and I did not wanted to see her sad. The exam continued for several hours, and I was feeling bit tensed too. I sat on one of the benches of the park and started chewing some bread-butter taken from the nearby cafeteria. All of my friends were busy with their own lives, and in the meantime, I saw Kartik. He was sitting under a tree and going through the brochure of Wipro Limited. I watched him flip the pages. His crooked eyebrows and intense gaze meant that he was preparing for the job and would be my potential competitor the very next day.

The clock struck two, and finally the examination was over. I sipped some water and then rushed to find Mansi. After around seven minutes, I found her. She was a bit dazed and was probably thinking about the solutions to some questions she had faced. I asked her how her exam went, and she replied that it was just fine. She told, "I don't expect much out of this anyway." I chuckled and replied, "Yeah. I don't expect much either." She smiled, and lightly hitting my left arm, replied, "Shut up! You are way smarter than me. This exam is a joke for you obviously." And then both of us smiled at each other. I gently held her hand and could feel her heart beating faster and faster, but suddenly, Neha popped in from behind all of a sudden and said, "Sooo! How was the exam..."

Quickly, Mansi let go of my hand and started talking to her. I thought it would be a good idea for me to leave, and thus waved her goodbye. All the way back home, I kept thinking about a girl who smiled very beautifully. I could still see her onyx eyes which could absorb all our gazes and carry us into some mystic land of wonders with no rain and no sorrow.

I was glued to the monitor screen as the results of the first round were to be declared sometime around midnight. I was praying for things to turn out the very best for a few of my friends. It was like Mansi made a wish and I crossed my fingers to make it come true. Long minutes of anticipation made me weary, and I started dozing. I was in the other part of the administrative block. Suddenly, at around 1:00 a.m., she called me, and with a tone of utter excitement exclaimed that she had been selected as a potential candidate. I was overjoyed and congratulated her. I was feeling so happy, as if I had conquered Mount Everest. Out of excitement, I could barely sleep that night, and Mansi was also very happy. She told me what type of questions had been asked and other stuff. She told me to prepare well so that I could get a job offer too. But, it's generally very tough for boys to slip through with an opportunity. After all, getting a job in that situation was like winning the Nobel Prize itself. So we kept talking for an hour. Our conversation always found something out of the blue to extend itself. I think that night I created record by talking over the phone continuously for four hours. My eyes were too tired, and I could feel that I was not in proper shape to give my best. I needed to sleep for a bit, and thus I told Mansi that I would talk to her later. It was six o'clock in the morning when I went to sleep. The next day, I woke up at nine, and was slightly scared because I had not prepared anything for the test. But I was confident enough. I checked my chat box and saw just a single message. It was from Mansi, and it went something like this:

"Manav!!! Wake up. It's already time. Come on. You are a genius, so don't worry too much. Best of luck, and remember to carry two extra pens along with you. And yes, make sure you eat something healthy in the morning."

That message boosted me a lot. I took a bath and set out with all my energy. I knew that the competition was going to be tough. Yet, I was confident because I knew I could do it.

The examination was over within a few hours, and I came outside in search of Kartik. I found Mansi there. She was waiting outside for Neha, and was reading some sort of a leaflet. I went to her and told her about the questions and how difficult they were. She smiled and asked, "How are you feeling now, Manav?" I said that I was fine, and then she started telling me about all sorts of things. She told me that there were placement opportunities in other companies, and that new companies were yet to come for special recruitment... Suddenly, Karan appeared out of the blue and asked Mansi to throw a party for getting placed in Wipro. The others joined him unanimously. Mansi found an excuse and said that she had to confirm the news first. But we were very excited that day. All of us went to the placement office and enquired about Mansi.

Yes! She had been placed in Wipro, and our party was on for sure. Everyone rushed towards the canteen, but I stayed there leaning against the hinge of the office door, thinking about what lay ahead. I looked at Mansi and she was looking at me. She raised her eyebrows with a sudden flicker and beckoned me to go to the canteen. I smiled a bit and then headed along with her.

It was almost 7:00 p.m. by the time we reached the canteen. We had some chips and soft drinks, but that failed to satisfy our happiness. Mansi understood that it was not enough, and promised to give another big party within a few days. Everyone wished her a great journey ahead. I was the happiest one among the lot, but I never exposed it in front of everyone. I had started liking her, but I kept my feelings within me.

On this planet, if you feel something, and even if you feel like you're being quite obvious about it, it doesn't translate until you actually show it. People tend to believe what they are shown. But sometimes, what we see and hear can be quite deceiving too. Even the sands beneath the ocean are cloaked by the high waves above it. I loved Mansi, and probably you, being the reader, might also have understood this fact. But whenever I tried to confess this truth with certain caring actions, Mansi showed opposite impulses. This agitated me a lot and sometimes, it became the reason for my quarrels with Mansi. We often had great clashes, and I sometimes used to test Mansi by remaining silent for a few days. I just wanted to see whether she really cared for me or not and whether she would try to cheer me up. Sometimes, I was rather prone to believe that she did not love me and that made me furious. I once decided not to talk to her and to stay away from her. It was like a one-sided, unofficial breakup, but I failed to keep it up for a long period of time. The thing is, it's very easy to forget someone who is not in contact with you. But our sight plays an important part in the inevitable delusion which allures us to dive once again into that pool of fantasy. If love is a gurgling stream, then quarrels are like small pebbles on the way. They provide resistance so that the force of love can increase just like that of the gushing waters flowing down from a mountain top.

My college life was about to wind up. The sun that day was high up in the blue sky. It was peeping through the clouds now and then, and its blazing beams fell on my shaggy graduation clothes. College was finally over, and I was about to enter the arena of practical life. Things were changing rapidly. Trust me, they have always kept changing from the very dawn of life. That day, we were all happy as well as sad. It was time to split ways and move in different directions, and we were taking each other's phone numbers and social network IDs. Some of us were still wandering in search of jobs, and others had been placed in companies like Wipro, NIIT, Mahindra, L&T, etc. We were all busy signing memoirs and penning down our summarised thoughts on diaries. All those stock phrases, boring lectures, canteen parties, broken hearts, complicated relationships, and above all, the friendships which had burnt their way into our minds, were the things we treasured the most. We had a get-together with all our professors and staff members. Everyone whom we had interacted with felt an ache in their heart. The strings of my heart had never before been pulled at so strongly. It was like we were standing in a circle, with our hands on each other's shoulders and dancing. Eventually, everyone went their own way, and I walked back home, skipping over the pavement with joy. It was evening, and the setting sun had flooded the sky with its goodbye hue. The birds were returning to their shelters, and so was I.

Half-Acceptance

As our classes were completed and I was waiting for my call from a company, I came back to my hometown for a few days to spend some time with my family: grandfather, grandma, and many others. I had been placed in Accel (an IT company), and was waiting for my joining date. Similar was the case with Mansi as well. She went back to Dehradun[12], also waiting for her joining date call from Wipro. But we used to text every day. One day, she informed me that she had received a call from Wipro.

"Hey topper! How are you?"

"Hey! I am fine. What about you?"

"I am not well. I have to go for document submission at Wipro the day after tomorrow, and I am super tensed."

Days of conversation had created a faint bridge of trust between us, and walking on that bridge, Mansi always told me all her problems. Moreover, I had started having serious feelings for her, and wanted her to share all her problems with me.

"So miss, what documents?"

"Nothing much, just the basic materials like marksheets, identification proofs, and birth certificate."

"So then what's there to be tensed about this?"

"I don't know. I am feeling uneasy. It's my first time. Try to understand the situation."

---

[12] City in the province of Uttarakhand

"Hmn. I get it ma'am."

"Actually the main problem is going there and then finishing the formalities on time. Like, I don't know the place quite well, that's why I asked for your help."

"Alright, don't worry. I shall go with you."

"Will that be a problem for you, because it's a long journey."

"No, it won't be any problem. Don't worry, I will be there."

"Thank you so much, Professor Sahab!"

"Oh Mansi! This is the least I could have done for you. And yes, don't say this thank you, because helping you is my pleasure."

"Alright, I take back my Thank You."

"Ha-ha-ha."

"So, what are you doing Mr?"

"Nothing much; just going through some stories of O. Henry."

"Hmn."

"What about you, miss?"

"I just said, I am just getting things ready."

"Good. So where are we going to meet?"

"Come down to the Meerut Cantt. station. I will meet you there.

"Alright Mansi, then this plan remains final."

"Yes! Going for dinner. Bye!"

"So early? Ok Good night then. I will meet you near the cantonment area the day after tomorrow. "

It was a usual Thursday morning, and the busy traffic honked its way past us as we paced towards the metro station. Mansi was wearing formal clothes that day, and her hair was tied in a bun. She was very anxious about her first day at Wipro, and I calmed her down by telling her that everything would be fine. There was quite a crowd in the metro station, and we had to muscle our way through it. I was holding her water bottle and documents while she went to fetch the tickets. Finally, we boarded our train to Delhi. We had to reach Okhla[13], New Delhi, where the Wipro office was. I convinced the ticket invigilator to allow us to board the AC compartment, but you know, nothing is for free in our country. So, I offered some bribe and finally we were in. Our compartment was air-conditioned, and that was really a relief. Mansi sat down on a vacant seat near the door and I stood clinging to the metal support near the door. She looked at me with tensed eyes and I smiled back to abate her fear. After two stations, the crowd thinned, and I eventually got the opportunity to sit beside her. I asked her about the cold and the crowd and did my best to distract her mind from thinking about the submissions and stuff. There was an oddly dressed lady sitting right opposite us, and I was mocking her dressing sense. Mansi started laughing and I felt a great relief in my heart. It took us another two hours to reach our destination.

Entering the main building of Wipro, we asked about the

---

[13] Okhla is a suburban colony located near Okhla barrage in South Delhi district of National Capital Territory of Delhi

submission process, and were told to go to the third floor. It was our first time were inside a corporate. The building was nicely maintained, very clean, with greenery all around, and the walls decorated with paintings, etc. But the lifts were out of order, and thus we had to use the stairs. There were other people too who had come for verification, and Mansi prepared to go inside through the glass door. I sat outside and started reading some journals. She told me that it would take some time, and thus I went downstairs to the cafeteria. I was roaming around in search of something out of the ordinary. After all, I had to spend my time somehow. Well, I was lucky. It did not take Mansi as long as I had expected. She returned within one o'clock, and we went to have lunch in the cafeteria. She was delighted as the verification process had been quite swift and hassle-free. It was great to see her smile like before. She went to the washroom to get refreshed, and I went through the menu card. Just as I was about to order my choice of food, I found Mansi with her hair untied. She was busy tucking her locks behind her ears and was looking radiant. That moment, I thought of telling her about my feelings for her, but suddenly she smiled back and asked me whether or not I had decided what to eat. Thrown off-guard, I said, "Oh yes! I have." In fact, I had not decided anything. The minutes rolled on with the food and the conversation, and all those barriers inside the heart remained firm. Every single moment, it was as if we were just strangers trying to know each other better, as if we were hoping for help from either end but were unable to express it directly.

Somewhere in the corner of my heart, I had started desiring for a life-partner like Mansi. But I knew that the path to our union would not be that easy. The path would be obviously riddled with difficulties, and I was prepared for anything serious. I knew that she would never leave me, and that was the very thing that comforted me during my toughest times. We were coming closer to each other every time Mansi sought my support, and were building a stronger bond of trust.

Discipline, being one of the most essential elements of life, is often hard to maintain. Although we had trained for it, we failed to attain it. Yes, during the last year of engineering, we all trained for SSB interview. SSB is the acronym for Services Selection Board, and it generally vets candidates for admission into the Armed Forces of India. So, we used to regularly get up early in the morning and go for warm-ups. We used to jog all around our campus, and it was really fun preparing for the Armed forces. Although we were never that serious about it, we kept on with our daily jogging routine. I was accompanied by Mansi, Pankaj, Karan and Gaurav. Doing something alone is quite monotonous. But when you do it in a group, you get involved in it and therefore tend to like it. When you tend to like it, obstacles can't hold you back, and when you can overcome any obstacle, you can actually succeed. It was a few months before our campus placement when we all boarded the train to Varanasi from Delhi. Our SSB selections were scheduled to be held in Varanasi, and we were all excited about it. I was a bit nosey and wanted to show my care for Mansi. I knew that she had trouble sleeping in trains and thus I kept myself awake too. As soon as the sun dipped into the horizon, we had our supper and everyone starting chatting with each other. I had nothing to say as such, and generally preferred to remain silent. After all, everyone can blabber nonsense; only few can keep their mouths shut and listen, right? The evening morphed into the night, and the sky blazed with stars. It was a wonderful sight and I will never be able to forget it. I had never seen so many stars in the night sky before. It seemed as if we were whirling round and round under the same dark roof, and the stars seemed like eyes, gazing lovingly at us from heaven. It was midnight and everything was wrapped in silence except the rattling of the wheels and the jerking of the railway sleepers. I was gazing at the night sky with my legs stretched out and my arms tucked by my sides. Suddenly, I saw Mansi coming. It was not a surprise for me, but still I made became a bit stiff. She looked at me and I smiled back as usual. I was trying to avoid her only to get her attention. I wanted her to break the ice this time. It was getting cold, but I enjoyed it. She came and sat opposite to me and said, "Why haven't you gone to sleep? It's quite late." This statement confused me a bit because, though it shows her care for me, it might also mean that she did not prefer my company. I was searching for a reply in my mind and ultimately said, "No. I am not feeling sleepy. It's good out here." And then we kept looking at each other and occasionally broke the eye contact to look outside the window. The moonlight fell on the trees and made the leaves glitter. The small pool of water and passing agricultural fields did make me a bit sleepy as well. We stayed there for about an hour and then she went inside the compartment. It was just a wonderful night.

The next day, we reached Varanasi early in the morning and came to know that our selection centre was 4 Air Force Selection Board[14]. At the station itself, we checked the

---

[14] Indian Air Force Officer's selection Centre

available rooms in hotels, and booked a separate, standard deluxe room for Mansi. We had our refreshments and then went to the SSB[15] centre, which was near the railway station, and started preparing for the first exam. The test was divided into two stages. We had to stay there for five more days after the Stage-1 test, which is also known as the PPDT[16] test. Fortunately, we all managed to clear the Stage-1 test. There was plenty of time in our hands, and hence we decided to tour the city of Varanasi. It was the month of August, and we had to tolerate the occasional drizzles on the way. I do not know about the others, but I enjoyed the rain. Our tests used to get over by 11 a.m., and after that we used to venture out into unknown streets just for the sake of adventure.

One fine morning, as I was standing on the veranda[17] and sipping my morning coffee, Mansi came and stood beside me. It was drizzling outside, and leaning against the wall, I was casually observing the light raindrops falling from far above onto the concrete floor. I smiled at her, and then we engaged in a random conversation about some general issues regarding our SSBs. Our batch was the only co-ed (combined) batch in which AFSB Varanasi had called for both boys and girls. There was a girl in the batch called Ruhi who was immensely beautiful and had captivating eyes. She was from Dalhousie, Himachal Pradesh, and was standing on the veranda just a yard beside me. I was often staring at her and Mansi saw this. I could see that Mansi was feeling uncomfortable. But she could not figure out why

---

[15] Services Selection Board, Army, Navy & Airforce officer's selection centre
[16] Picture Perception and Description Test, first test of the selection Process
[17] A raised, covered, sometimes partly closed area, often made of wood, on the front or side of a building

she was feeling so. She was annoyed and left the place in agitation. I left the place too and went after her.

Finally, on the 5th day, our results were declared. To our shock and dismay, none of us were selected. However, Gaurav and I had another interview just the next day. I passed the interview and was a step ahead, but eventually felt deserted on that SSB selection portal as Mansi had left. I did not pause for a moment to take a clear decision, and thus I too went back to Delhi with all of my friends.

After the havoc of the SSBs, I moved into Shipra Sun City[18], a residential society where all of my roommates were staying and searching for jobs. We rented a two-room flat there. We enjoyed a lot in that period of time. Sometimes, on various friend's birthday, we were accompanied by Upasana and Mansi as well. There was excitement in the air, and slowly but steadily, the news regarding Mansi and Manav started to spread. I became pretty sure about it. One day, all roommates planned to play a game: the game of spinning the bottle. When the bottle stopped pointing towards me, everyone bombarded me with questions regarding Mansi. It was quite annoying at first, because I had tried to keep the fact as confidential as possible. But you know, friends, they always get a hint of what goes on in your life.

After six months of leaving college, I started feeling those flickers of uncertainty. Life became like a dreary desert without those moments of fun and enjoyment. Like everyone else, I was missing my college days too. The best thing that had ever happened to me in those four years

---

[18] One of the posh societies in the city

(especially in the final year) was Mansi. She filled my life with various colours. Whenever I used to be upset regarding something, she used to drop in from nowhere and bring a smile to my face. There was not a single wakeful moment in our lives when we did not miss each other. We were in love. Deep love! Although she never expressed it directly, deep down in my heart, I could feel her care for me and knew that she had feelings for me. We used to stay up talking late nights on a daily basis, and I used to drop Mansi at her office and pick her up at the end of the day. Sometimes she used to drive and sometimes I took the wheel. One certain day, Mansi was too tired from the day's work to drive, and could barely keep her eyes open. Therefore, I was driving that day and she was sitting beside me. Her seat was a bit reclined, and she was lying on it, comfortably snuggled. I glanced at her while waiting at a signal post; her eyes were closed and her hair was strewn all over her temple. I drove as carefully as I could, avoiding all the bumps and ridges on the way. Whenever I saw her sleeping in peace or smiling with joy, I felt as if I had conquered something very special. It was kind of a blessing for me to see her happy.

After a few months, Mansi was posted in Iqor Inc., which meant that she had to go for work early in the morning. I was highly annoyed with this because her work came in between our late night talks, and eventually I had to wish her Good night by 10 p.m. The problem was that my body had become conditioned to remain awake till late at night, and a sudden shift in schedule completely disrupted it. I had difficulty in sleeping, and every now and then switched on my smartphone to go through our chats. I barely slept for four hours and got up at 6:30 so that I could talk to

Mansi once before dropping her off at work. She remained busy with her work throughout the day and I had to figure out something to keep myself busy. But the most delightful fact was that there were a lot of important things to keep myself engaged. Mansi had got a job and I had still not managed to get one. This was the very thing which bugged me every moment. I was quite frustrated with my life and my choices. When I was young, at about the age of 13, I enjoyed reading the daily magazine which came in with our morning newspaper. It contained crossword puzzles and various fun facts which never failed to entertain me. The magazine also published the thought for the day, and once I read a quote that went something like this:

"We are humans, and are emotional beings. Hence, we must always

make sure to control our emotions lest they control us..."

But I could never define the difference between being emotional and being in love. Because love, for me, was like an emotional adventure. It was like a maze, which when entered once, ought to be completed.

It was Friday night and I could still feel the anxious anticipation which ran though my spine as I saw Mansi typing something on the chat window.

"Hey! How was your day, prof?"

"Yeah, nothing out of the ordinary. How was your day at work?"

"Well, it was fine. Same old duty-driven day."

"Hmn. So how are you?"

"I am fine. How are you?"

"I am fine, Jaanu."

"Jaanu???"

"Ha-ha. Sorry."

"Why sorry Mr?"

"Cause I told you that. Ha-ha."

"Accha... really?"

"Yeah really."

"Ha-haa."

"Hmn...madam."

"Hey Manav, I wanted to tell you something serious."

"Yeah, go ahead."

"What will happen if you come to know that someone whom you love the most is not faithful and loyal to you?"

"What does that even mean?"

"I mean, if you come to know that someone you love has done something wrong, I mean, if she has crossed her limits with some other person?"

I was shocked at this, and although I could sense the gravity of the situation, I could hardly believe what I was reading. I got highly irritated with this and replied, "So what is the matter???"

"Ohh sir! Matter is anything which occupies space and has dimensions."

"Wao!!!! Really??? I was completely unaware of this. Thank you for telling me."

"Ha-ha!!!!"

"So are you please going to say the actually thing?? Please!!"

"Yeah. The thing is that I did something in Iqor."

"What?"

"Something I think I should not have done."

"Then why did you do it?"

"Try to understand. It's a type of requirement or need."

"What???!!!!! Requirement or need?????!!! What the heck?"

"I am sorry, Manav."

"Sorry???? Is this a joke or something????"

"I knew that you would react like this."

"What??? Oh really?? And as if I thought that you would do something like what you did. This is so disgusting."

"Calm down Mr..."

"Oh yes...yes...yes. Of course, why not? I will have to calm down now."

"What is the matter?"

"Matter is something which occupies space and eats up the heart and brain madam!!!"

"Ooo..."

"Please. Please. I don't wanna talk right now. Good night. I've got to sleep."

"Hey wait. It's not that late. You can't sleep now."

"Oh I am really sorry, Ms. Mansi. It's kind of a requirement, please try to understand."

I was so frustrated by the situation that I immediately switched off the mobile data and cuddled with my pillow. I lay still on my bed, thinking of the mistake that I had made for all these months. My phone was in silent mode and thus I could not get to know that Mansi had called me seven times. When I discovered this, it was already ten minutes late, and I never wanted to contact her ever. But my foolish heart persuaded my mind to call her. The first time, the call remained unanswered, but then she picked up. She was furious with me and said, "Why didn't you pick up my call, huh?? So this is what you think of me, huh???" I felt a bit guilty and remained silent. Mansi kept yelling, "I just said this to see whether you trust me or not." I was thinking what to say because I was totally confused. I had never prepared myself for such an awkward circumstance. Although I was still angry, as minutes passed by, I started feeling guilty. I gathered all my courage and answered, "But you must understand that I trust you too much; that is why I believed you in the first place." There was a moment of silence and then she tenderly giggled a bit, switched to her soft tone, and replied, "Mad boy!" I had never heard something so caring and full of love. I smiled and she smiled and soon both of us broke into laughter which eventually died down. But for the next few days or weeks, those words of hers were stuck in my mind. Coming back to the moment, we were silent, completely silent, connected to each other through the endless dimension of love. Suddenly, the clock struck three and broke our silence. "Manav, let's go to sleep now. I am feeling sleepy," said Mansi. I replied, "Body requirement, huh?" I could hear a snatch of laughter from the other end. I could hear the wall clock ticking in the deathly silence of the room. Sleep had caught hold of my eyes too, and hearing the reply, I felt a bit guilty. I wanted to keep talking to her; I wanted to be with her and take care of her. But the distance between us was impassable. I wanted to tell her a thousand things but could not manage to keep her awake. My eyes were getting heavier with each second and I eventually replied in a tone of utmost care and love, "Yes Madam, let's go to sleep."

After a few days, luck brought us a very soothing coincidence. Mansi did not have work that day and I was free too; so we decided to visit Akshardham[19]. It was the nearest tourist spot from our residence and thus we chose to go there. Akshardham is a very good picnic spot and attracts a lot of people every day. The main temple is surrounded by beautiful gardens where one could walk on the green grass and sit under the open sky. Mansi and I held each other's hands and walked on the paved path along the green patches of grass. It was a gleeful morning and butterflies were dancing in the mild breeze which carried the scent of the blooming flowers. I looked at her and she looked at me and it seemed as if time had frozen forever. Her warm hands were moist and I could feel that something was bugging her from inside. We kept walking for the next few minutes and talked about the greenery of the place and how it had been inaugurated by Dr. A.P.J. Abdul Kalam. There were other people too, but fortunately, there was no crowd that day. After a while, Mansi and I decided to go and sit on the wooden benches that faced the temple. As we sat, Mansi clasped my left hand

---

[19] Akshardham or Swaminarayan Akshardham complex is a Hindu temple, and a spiritual-cultural campus in Delhi, India.

and rested her head on my shoulder. I could feel that she was sad. I put my hand on her cheek and said, "What is the matter? Why are you gloomy?" She refrained from telling me anything and her silence made me restless. But this was not the first time I was facing such a circumstance. I was used to these small pauses in our conversation and thus turned my attention to the blue sky and the chirping birds on the trees. Finally, she broke the silence and said, "It is not possible..." I was taken aback and asked, "What is not possible?" She left my hand and replied, "This, our relationship, is not possible. Our families have stark differences and my parents would never accept this." Suppressing my inner conflict, I assured her that everything would fall into place with time and that my parents would talk to her parents when the right time arrived. I took her hand and drew the letter 'I' on her palm. "See, now there is no one who can separate us. I have carved myself on your palm. Don't worry miss...we are made for each other." Mansi smiled and said, "My mad boy!"

We kept talking to each other and our ignited minds failed to keep track of time. She was chattering like a parrot and her wet, red lips, like the beak of a parrot, glistened as sunlight struck them. When the setting sun waved its last goodbye, we got up and went to see the musical fountain.

The musical fountain is the crown jewel of Akshardham. It is the largest step-well in India, and consists of 2,870 steps and hundred and eight small shrines from which jets of water gush into the lotus having eight petals at the centre. I was standing there, contemplating the beautiful display of colours and enjoying the soothing music when suddenly, Mansi pulled my hand and took me near to the fountain. I had never seen her so happy; she held my hands and we sat near the foamy spray of water. I looked straight at her and said "Mansi, I wanted to…" My mouth went completely dry and I froze. My hands started trembling.

She asked, "What happened, Manav?"

"Mansi, I think I'm falling for you and would like to be a part of my life. If you don't feel the same, please don't feel offended and please don't leave. We can still be good friends.

"No Manav, my parents would not agree at all. Our parents will not be comfortable with this relationship."

I was half-relieved, half-disappointed by her half-acceptance. After having a long conversation, we realized that it was already late and we should leave. The deep blue sky was filled with twinkling stars and the moon was bright in the sky. Within an hour, we were half-drenched and decided to return home. I dropped Mansi at her paying guest and drove back home. It was one of the most memorable evenings of my life. Mansi and I started spending a lot of time with each other, frequenting movie halls or just hanging out together.

December came to an end and it was the last day of the month. I was texting Mansi, and there were just a day and a few hours left for 2009 to begin. The next day, we made plans for a New Year's celebration somewhere in Delhi and were discussing something regarding that. Mansi requested me to wear a grey shirt and black trousers, and also mentioned that I looked handsome in grey clothes. I never had the peculiar taste of dressing sense that she had, and thus remained quiet on this particular topic. She wanted me to suggest something for her to wear, and I just bluntly replied that anything she wore would look good on her. The intention of my reply was to praise her beauty, but she caught it in a tone of utter frustration. She complained that I had no sense of art and that I should work on my aesthetic skills a bit. You know, our conversation always took us into a virtual world where time had no existence. Thus, we nearly forgot that we had entered into the new year two minutes back. It was 12:02 a.m. when Mansi sent me, "Mad boy! Happy New Year 2009." I had no time to ponder over my foolishness and replied immediately, "Mah girl, Happy New Year 2009." Although I had wanted to wish her first, it did not matter much because I was overjoyed to have her wish me first. The next day was going to be a hectic one, and thus we mutually agreed to end our conversation there itself. We wished each other Good night and went to sleep.

The next day, I woke up early in the morning, took a shower and wore that grey shirt which Mansi had suggested. I combed my hair, and for the first time in my life, applied hair gel. Some of you might think that it was for impressing Mansi, but it was because of the tendency of my hair was to go haphazard, and I could not bear seeing it in that state that day. I called Mansi a couple of times but she did not pick up. I assumed she was busy dressing up and thus headed for her destination. When I was halfway there, my phone rang and it was Mansi. I took the call and in a tone of utter deference said, "Good Morning ma'am. Are you awake or still in the land of your dreams?" Mansi was eating something and said, "What is this? I said that we would go out at 8 o'clock. It's already 8:25, where are you?" I was astonished by her reply and thought of utilizing this moment to play a small trick on her. I said with a yawn, "Oh God!

I am going to take my bath now. Please wait dear. I will be there within another thirty minutes." I took care of every other detail except for the fact that I was standing beside the road and the honking of the cars could be prominently heard over the call. Mansi giggled a bit and asked whether I was going to take a bath on the road or in a nearby public washroom. I laughed and said, "Wait, I am already halfway there. I will be there soon." You know the nature of Ms. Mansi. She would never let you cut the call without adding an ending touch to it. I wished her "bye!" and was about to cut the call when she interrupted, "Wait...wait...wait... Drive slowly; there is no need to rush. Otherwise, I am pretty sure you will bump into a car and then the driver will accuse me for the accident." I could not control my laughter and promised her that the driver wouldn't accuse her for anything. She wished me good luck and cut the call. When I reached her place, I found her in an white attire. She was looking so sweet that I could not resist myself from taking her picture. She came towards me with angry eyes and enquired, "Where is your helmet?? Where is it?" I had applied gel on my hair and that is why I did not wear the helmet. But I could not possibly say that to her. She was furious with me and refused to go with me until I wore the helmet. I tried to convince her to believe that nothing unfortunate would happen with me but she remained so stubborn that I had to finally accede to her request. We enjoyed a lot that day. We drove for miles and miles, drank roadside tea, attended a party in one of the restaurants in Spice Mall, and sang all the way back to our respective residences. I was tired after the day's adventures and thus clung to the bed for the next few hours. It was nearly nine o'clock when Mansi called me and said that she was feeling lonely. I was half-asleep and so could not understand the depth of the situation. Mansi kept speaking for sometime and then disconnected the call. I remember one instance, while leaving in the morning, Pankaj had wished me that my wish would come true that day and laughed. After about one hour, I woke up, and to my horror, found nineteen missed calls from Mansi. I quickly left my bed, washed my face, and called Mansi. I called five consecutive times but she did not pick up. I was tensed and kept calling. After the seventh trial, she picked up the call and said, "I don't wanna talk to you." Her anger was justifiable and I apologized. She said, "Yes... yes... No, I am sorry for disturbing you. I am really very sorry." Apart from cracking the UPSE exams, the next hardest thing to do in India is to coax an angry girl, and the task becomes even harder when the girl is your girlfriend. So, I kept on apologizing and flooded her chat box with loads of sorry's. After sometime, I became fed up and thus stopped texting her. I was waiting for her to reply but she did not. Hours passed and I kept waiting in anticipation. Finally, after midnight, she replied. The only reason she could give for such a delayed reply was that she had been angry the previous day and she had been waiting for the day to get over. Fair and square!

I started dialling her number but I was afraid. I did not know how to start the conversation and always had the fear that I might mess things up. The phone started ringing and then came the sweetest sound which still rings in my ears. The "Hello" had some magic in it. It was so soothing and soft that it was like the sound of a dove. Her voice bewitched me and I eventually replied with a heavy "HELLO!" We started giggling and talking our hearts out. Her voice had a jolly note. She said, "So, Mr. Manav. Why did not you pick up my call?" I did not want to rekindle the fire which had recently been put out. Thus, I said, "I am really sorry dear. I was so tired that I fell asleep. I am very very sorry. It was not at all intentional." She giggled a bit and said, "It's ok dear. I could understand."

The conversation which followed was a weird one:

"Why were you feeling lonely dear?"

"It was nothing. I often feel lonely, sir."

"I am always there with you... Just tell me when you feel sad. I will make you happy."

"Yeah Mr...Just don't fall asleep."

"Hmn...Lol."

"Ha-ha!"

"Today was fun, wasn't it?"

"Yeah. It was great."

"I loved the entire day."

"Hmn. I enjoyed it too. Hey, I wanted to tell you something important."

"Yeah, tell me."

"It's like a question sort of."

"Yeah, go ahead."

"You must answer it honestly."

"Yes, I will try."

"No, you have to. It's important."

"Ok! I will. Now tell me the thing."

"I texted you."

The notification bell rang and there was the message:

"Do you really love me, and if it's a yes, then how much?"

I replied, **"Yes, it's true. 100%."**

"Oh! Really?"

"Yes. Really."

I felt like holding her tight in my arms and gently pecking her lips. My heart was thumping faster as I asked her, "Now you answer me the same question, but if percentage is greater than zero, then say "yes" & how much. Do you love me, and if it's a yes, then how much?"

The call suddenly got cut. Minutes had turned into hours and I had been oblivious to the fact that the balance of my phone was getting exhausted. It had completely run out and this made me terribly sad. I thought of recharging my phone when suddenly I saw the clock showing the time as 11:00 p.m. That day, I understood the pain of having a nearly full network connection and battery power and still unable to enjoy talking to someone special over the phone.

I immediately opened up the chat box and could see the typing logo flash up on the screen. It came up and then disappeared. Mansi was typing and erasing something and I was not sure why she was doing that. I expected the answer to be quite a straightforward one, but what I read was somewhat different.

She wrote,

"Yes! I do love you. 40 percent..."

I was perplexed and could not resist myself from asking her the reason for such a passive answer. However, she dodged my question and requested me to say something cheerful. We wished each other, and the rest of the night of 1st January, 2009 passed by in charming conversation. Our conversation always found something out of the blue to extend itself. I think that night I made the Guinness World Record for talking over the phone continuously for six hours. It was nearly 4 a.m. when Mansi proposed to go to sleep. I chuckled and replied, "Really? Now you wanna go to sleep?? It's already dawn." She said, "Yes, at least for an hour or two." Thus we wished each other "Good Morning" and went to sleep.

Before dropping Mansi at her office, we went to the Kalkaji Mandir[20] that day. We used to visit that temple quite often and made religious offerings like normal couples. Even before we proposed to each other, we used to go to that temple and pray during the exams. Time had created an inevitable bond between us and that temple. Mansi told me once that if I really wanted her in my life, then I should devote vermilion to the lord. From that day onwards, I willingly did the same. Whenever I devoted vermilion, the priest used to return me a portion of it and I used to give that to Mansi. That day, we both were standing in front of the idol with folded hands when the priest came to me and handed over the remaining vermilion. He smiled at me,

---

[20] Kalkaji Mandir, also known as Kalkaji Temple, is a Hindu mandir or temple, dedicated to a Hindu Goddess

and using his fingers, indicated me to apply that portion on Mansi's forehead. Mansi was still praying, with her hands folded. I took a pinch of the vermillion and applied it on her hairline instead of her forehead. Mansi suddenly opened her eyes and looked upwards to inspect what had happened. When she discovered the vermilion on her hairline, she took a pinch of it from my hands and applied it on my cheeks. I smiled back and kissed her on her forehead. She whispered in my ears, "This is a temple..." And we both giggled for a moment. Mansi had office that day and thus she was annoyed with the mark on her hairline. She went to the washroom to get rid of that mark while I stood at the entrance with her bag. Generally, we had to stand in a long queue before getting a chance to worship, but that day the crowd was light and we did not have to stand for long. When Mansi came back, I took out my handkerchief and offered it to her. She took it and dried her hairline. A thin mark was still visible, but it was of negligible intensity. From that point of time, we both started considering ourselves as a married couple. Mansi used to fast on "Karvachauth" (it is a one-day festival celebrated by Hindu women in Northern India, in which married women fast from sunrise to moonrise for the safety and long life of their husbands) and she didn't even take a drop of water. In the evening, looking at the full moon, she would touch my feet. We would hug and then have dinner together. Such things started thappening since then.

After dropping Mansi at her office in Okhla, I returned to my residence and started studying for one of my upcoming exams.

The biggest problem in life is our inability to create a sense of alertness at the right time. That is exactly what happened to me. Although everything seemed to run perfectly on the relationship front, I was still not satisfied with my professional life. A piece of the puzzle was missing, and hence I took a firm resolve to go for an MBA. Whatever I did in my life, I discussed it with Mansi so that I could know her opinion on the matter too. When I told her about my decision to pursue MBA from Amity University, she became excited and wanted to take the course along with me. However, this never materialized since I had my exams just a weeks from then, and Mansi was completely unprepared. Thus, we mutually decided that she would join from the next year. Although I had not secured my position in any of the colleges, I automatically felt like a senior. I was very happy that day. My happiness was not because I was going to do an MBA, it was because Mansi was accompanying me in that venture. Somewhere down the road, few nodes of my happiness were entangled with Mansi's. Whenever she felt happy, I felt bliss.

So, I gave the exam and eventually got into Amity University. For most part of the first year, things were quite drab for me. Long lectures and hectic assignments burdened all of us. However, the next year, Mansi joined a part-time course. She had her duties and so it was a bit harder for her to cope with all these stipulated time frames. She trusted me a lot and hence, sometimes, I completed her assignments and made sure that her fees were paid in due time. There was something really crazy about that time period. Both of us were so much engaged in our lives that we seldom found time for each other. Although we talked for hours at night, it was never enough. Sometimes we used to sit in the canteen and do our assignments. I had made a couple of friends in my first year and they were all annoyed with me because, from the second year, I never paid enough attention to them. They had their regular complaints like, "relationship steals away friendship." Although I was not completely against this view, I just saw it from a different perspective. To me, love had the greatest priority in life, and when that love was meant for someone special, I found it obligatory to give it a special position in my life as well. The whole college knew about us, and thus we did not have the pressure of keeping things clandestine. However, there was one thought which kept bugging inside me: the thought of Mansi's parents. Whenever such thoughts came in my mind, I somehow suppressed them by consoling myself with optimistic ideas. I loved Mansi, and she loved me too, but there was some annoying intuition which beckoned my mind to think of the worst possible outcomes. I could never make my way out of these haunting thoughts and always kept thinking about possible solutions to such problems. One day, while we were walking down to the conference hall, Mansi suggested that we sit on the green grass of the open field and do our assignment. The plan was quite an interesting one. The sun was glistening through the clouds that day and many others were sitting on the field too. After an hour or so, Mansi pulled my left hand and started drawing the outline of my veins with a pen. I could sense that she was in deep thought and hence asked her the reason for it. She hesitated at first, but then replied, "Manav, what will happen if my parents do not accept our relationship?" I don't know why, but I said in a humorous tone that we would elope and marry each other. When she heard this, she left my hand and said in an angry tone, "I would never do that. If we marry, then it would be with the consent of our parents." I looked up at her and with a smile said, "Oh my Princess, nothing will happen. At least my parents will never say no. I don't know about your parents. You will have to convince them," I said. She remained silent and I could not bear to see her in that state. I pulled her closer and kissed her on her forehead. I rolled my lips near her ears and whispered, "We are made for each other. You are my sweet little wife." She took her right hand and showed that spot on her palm where I had written the letter 'M' with my fingers. She said, "Look Manav! You are here." I held her hand, kissed her palm, and promised to stay there forever.

After three long years, the day finally arrived when I graduated as an MBA. It was our convocation day, and Mansi was present there. Although she had her office that day, she took out some time for me. Mansi was very happy that day, and she kept taking snaps all through the congregation. We had a small party followed by the felicitation ceremony. After that, I dropped Mansi at her office and then returned back to the college to join the other arrangements. It was a day of total enjoyment and freedom.

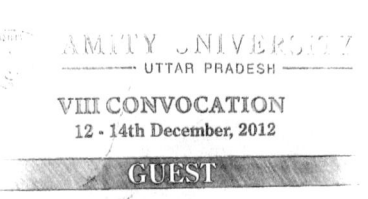

After just a few months, Mansi had her convocation, and I was present there. Mansi's sister, Shweta, had also come to attend her convocation, and she was staring at me every now and then. It was quite tough for me to hold in my emotions when Mansi was awarded the degree. I cheered for her and took a lot of photographs. The main purpose of taking the photographs was to present Mansi with a beautiful collage so that she could keep the memories of our MBA program safe forever. Hence, a week after the convocation, I bought a collage frame and meticulously pasted the photos one after the other in such a haphazard way that ultimately, they made a chain of events. It was like a string carrying all our memories of the New Year Bike ride as well as the MBA programme. When I presented Mansi with that collage, she was so overjoyed that she hugged me tight and kissed me on the cheeks. She said, "Oh Manav, I love you so much..." I wrote a message on that collage as well, which went something like this:

"Mansi, you have achieved a great success. You are brilliant, able and ambitious. I bless you with all that you need to earn many more achievements. You dreamt, you believed, you strived and you achieved. Congratulations on your Convocation... -Manav"

Don't Let Me Down

What is being mature? Or rather, let me put it in this way: how do you judge someone to be mature? It's nothing but their ability to resolve issues that they face. It is said that life is 1 percent of what happens to us and 99 percent of how we react to those unexpected situations. And when we grow up, our responsibilities begin to pileup. They make us more conscious of our existence and successfully bind us into this amazing portrait of life. But, the real dilemma strikes in our minds when we start realizing the fact that nothing is permanent in life and attaching ourselves to something mortal is quite horrific. It not only puts us in the path of the misfortune of losing someone special, but also drives us into thinking about the future with such ferocity that we ultimately lose our present moment.

I call still hear the crunching of those dried leaves under the tyres of my motorcycle as I rode towards Mansi's residence to pick her up. It was a Monday, and the sun's rays had warmed up the surrounding air, which brought with itself a tinge of chill. The wheels of my motorbike gleefully raced along the broadway as I mirthfully hummed the classical tune of a song from a movie Ghazini, which was about to be released in a few months. Mansi always complained about my timing sense, and according to her, I was seldom punctual. That day, I woke up early in the morning so that I could make myself ready and reach her hostel at the exact dot of the second. On the way, I was thinking about her and was predicting the colour of her dress that she would be wearing. However, when I reached her residence, I was perplexed to see that she was not waiting for me on the spot where she usually did. I glanced at my watch and found that I was exactly on time. I waited for another 10 minutes then I decided to call her up. The first couple of times she did not pick up the call; then, suddenly, she peeped from the window and came down running. She was in her ordinary clothes and had applied something on her hand. I was worried about her and immediately asked her about the bluish layer of cream which was on her left hand. She said that while she was preparing that morning's tea, the warm water accidently slipped from the kettle and fell on her hand. She saw that I was worried and thus assured me that nothing serious had happened. I requested her to make some arrangements so that I could at least stay with her for that day; but she said that making such accommodations was near impossible because it was a girls' hostel and the entry of boys was strictly prohibited. I was in a fix! I could neither go to my work nor get inside and help Mansi with her work. However, I went to work after hearing from Mansi that there were some other girls in her room who would return from the market soon. I requested her to call me once those girls returned so that I could at least be sure that she was not left all by herself. My adamant heart was not letting me go to work. Mansi pulled my hand and took me to the waiting room. When we were inside, she held my hands and kissed on my knuckles. Then she slowly told me, "Go to work, I shall be fine." I held her for the first time; I kissed her on her forehead. There was some magic in that moment and we could not resist ourselves from that intoxicating flow. I could feel her breath on my lips and then we kissed each other for the first time. My heart was beating faster than ever. Mansi put one of her hands on my shoulder and ran the fingers of the other through my hair. I could feel the fresh smell of her mouth and the fissures on her lips. When we drew apart, I saw Mansi's hair in sixes and sevens. My hair was in the same condition too, and I had to do my hair up using my hands so that I could leave for work. I took Mansi's other palm and said, "Take care of yourself. I will come again after six o'clock. And yes, don't forget to give me a call once your friends return from the market." She kept staring at me and then slowly, her tensed face broke into a beautiful smile. She said, "Drive safely, mad boy. Or else, I am quite sure that you will bump into a vehicle and that driver will accuse me of not warning you to drive slowly." I smiled and asked, "Why? Why will the driver accuse you? There are a lot of girls in this planet. Why only you?" She came closer to me and looking into my eyes said, "Because I am a mad girl and you are a mad boy. Now go to work..." Our conversation ended in smiles and then I left for work.

Although I went to work, I could never concentrate properly. My supervisor became so annoyed with me that he eventually said, "Mr. Newcomer! Where is your mind? What's the problem? It seems that you have not settled yet. Better get your mind here or else I am afraid we won't be able to pull you through." Our manager was a good-natured person but he had his reasons for indirectly blackmailing me. From the very second I entered into the office that day, after every hour, I checked my phone for missed calls or other message notifications. After four hours had passed, I became quite restless and finally called Mansi. She picked up the call and I could hear other voices, possibly of her roommates. I asked her, "Why did not you call me? I was a little worried." She did not get it at first, but then said, "I am sorry, dear. I fell asleep and then when I woke up, I had forgotten about the call." I was very happy to hear that and said, "It's ok jaanu. Take care."

While coming back from work, I bought some fruits and a soothing gel for her. It was nearly 6:40 p.m. when I rang her up and she came down. She had applied some ice-pack on her hand, and it looked far better than before. I told her to call one of her friends so that she could help her carry those fruits and other essential things to the room. When I came home, I called her up and asked her whether she needed anything. She said, "Yes! You." Ina tone of utter disbelief I said, "Accha! Really??" And then the conversation went on for a couple of hours. I really did not want to burden her that day and thus requested her to go to sleep. But she refused to leave and wanted to keep talking. Thus, I said, "Ok! But only for another thirty minutes." She got agitated with this reply and said, "No need mister. It's better we go to sleep. Good night." By the time I could comprehend my actual mistake, she hung up the call and sent me a 'Good night' message. I did not want to stir things up and thus went to sleep with the hope that her mood would be better by the next day.

The next morning, when I went to pick up Mansi, I found her sitting on a bench adjacent to her hostel, reading the newspaper. To draw her attention, I rang the horn and then parked my bike and went and sat beside her. She was looking gorgeous as usual, wearing a velvet scarf and a pink attire. She looked at me and then raised her eyebrows to indicate that we should leave for office. I gave her the extra helmet and off we went, along with the morning breeze. On the way to Mansi's office, we had to ride on the Yamuna river bridge, which is also known as the DND flyway. This was the place where we used to halt for a few minutes and drink tea on the roadside from a nearby stall. Back then, I did not have a smartphone or a smart-camera. So, I often used my old photo film camera to capture those moments. Although Mansi often complained that I remained busy with my camera and seldom paid attention to the surroundings, I always dodged her complaint with a smile. One day, she became so agitated that she snatched the camera from my hands and was about to throw it away, but I somehow saved it after a lot of arguments. Whenever Mansi did not feel well but had to attend her office, I used to drop her at her workplace and also took care of all her medicines.

Mansi had sinusitis problems for a long time, due to which she sometimes suffered from severe headaches. This annoyed her a lot and did not let her concentrate on her job. At that time, there was a very well-known doctor named Bhatnagar in New Delhi. He had immense expertise in the field of Homeopathic medicines, and was also a health consultant to the President of India then. I somehow convinced Mansi to go for a check-up, and soon after that she felt a lot better. It gave me great joy to see her healthy and happy.

One day, Mansi called me up and said that she was going to her hometown, Dehradun. She said, "Manav! I am going home for a few days." The news was so sudden that I had no time to ask her for more details like the train tickets and other things. I said, "So, you going by train?"

"Yup!"

"How many days, dear?"

"Not much. May be five weeks."

"Hmn! So more than a month."

"Don't worry. We would talk."

"Hmn...So what about the tickets?"

"I have booked the tickets and my sister would be there on the platform. So don't worry."

"So, when are you leaving?"

"Tomorrow evening."

"Hmn. I am going to drop you then."

"Yesss Manav!! Of course."

"Hey girl, can I ask you something?"

"Sure..."

"Are you going to say anything regarding me to your mom?"

"No! Not now. I don't think this is the right time."

"Ok! So when are you gonna tell her?"

"I will tell her when she talks to me regarding these things."

"Which things?"

"I mean these things like boys and marriage."

"What if she has already thought of someone for you?"

"Look, I know my mom very well. She won't do anything against my preference."

"Hmn. But what if she tells you to leave me?"

"She would never tell that. And yes, I won't leave you."

"Why??"

"I know my mom very well."

"No, I mean, why won't you leave me??"

"Because I am mad and you are mad."

"Acchaa??"

"Yes, mad boy!"

"Hey! You know nah that I love you so so so much."

"No, heard this for the first time, sir."

"Accha!"

"Haha... I love you too sweetheart...Buh-bye!"

"Bye!"

The next day, I picked up Mansi and bought some snacks for her so that she would have some something to eat on her way back home. At dusk, she called me and said that her train was at 9:00 p.m. I left early from my office and went to pick her up at six o'clock. She was ready with her luggage and asked me to help her load them in the cab. Mansi was a bit worried about the evening traffic, but I assured her that we would reach on time. Eventually, we did reach way before time, but there was a big crowd at the station and we had a tough time searching for our platform and coach number. After waiting for another thirty minutes or so, the train arrived and Mansi boarded it. I was a bit worried about her, and thus wanted to talk to her over the phone through the entire train journey. When she heard this proposal, she smiled and said, "Why do you worry about me so much? I will be fine…" She took my right hand and, kissing it, said, "Take care of yourself. And yes, don't forget to wear the helmet while on the bike…"

We talked for a few more minutes and then I bid her good bye. She was a bit nervous and so was I. Those days, it was very tough, nearly impossible for me to pass a month without talking to her. But there was no alternative to this, and she had to leave. The train whistled and pulled off. With every step that I took away from the platform, my heart became heavier.

When I reached home, I called Mansi, "Hello Ma'am. So how are you?"

"Not well."

"Hey, why? ☹"

"Because you are not here."

"Accha. So should I come?"

"Yes, come fast."

"Well, I am there, sitting just beside you."

"There is an old man who is sitting beside me, so is it you??"

"No…"

"Haha. So where are you?"

"I am there sitting inside your heart."

"Oooo…"

"Hmnn… So madam, when will you have dinner?"

"I will have it now…"

"Ok... Is everything alright? I mean, are you facing any sort of problem?"

"Yes... Everything is alright, my Manav... Don't worry about me."

"I have to, because I love you I think."

"Hey, dinner is here. Ok bye... Good night."

"Alright, eat well and then go to sleep. If you have any trouble then let me know. Good night and sweet dreams, love."

"Good night...sweet dreams. You have your dinner right now too. Then we would be having our dinner together."

"Hmn I am going right now."

"Bye Manav..."

"Buh-bye!"

For the next few weeks, we kept talking over the phone and social media. Mansi's absence made me somewhat restless. For the last few months, I had developed such a soft corner for her in my heart that my happiness and my expectations had become entangled with hers. I counted the days and waited for her arrival. Finally, the day of her return dawned. I was overjoyed and decided to get a small gift for her at the railway station. Her train was on time and I greeted her with a smile as she alighted. I immediately took her luggage from her hands and started a random conversation with her. I asked her about her parents' health, the journey, and her stay in Dehradun. When we got inside the car, I took out arose and a card from my bag and handed them over to her. She was surprised and hugged me tight. She kept holding me and said, "I felt so lonely out there. I missed you so much." I said, "Mansi, please never

ever have second thoughts in your mind, because now things have changed." She held my palm even tighter. The pain of her long absence vanished into thin air, and I felt as if nature had bestowed all her comfort on me. That day, after returning home, we talked till late at night about some important things regarding our work and then went to sleep.

The next day, when I woke up, I called Mansi and asked her what she was doing. She seemed busy and said in a tone of frustration, "Neha and I are cooking toast and sandwiches."

I giggled a bit and asked, "How?"

"What do you mean how?"

"I mean, with what utensils?"

"Ooo. Nothing extraordinary, mister. Just simple cooking utensils."

"Oh! That's quite tough then."

"Hmn. And what about you? Did you wake up just now?"

"Haha. Unfortunately, yes!"

"Ok... I am hanging up now. Will talk later."

"Ok bye!"

"Bye!"

Hearing that Mansi was struggling to make toast and sandwiches, I decided to gift her a toastmaker and a juicer-mixer-grinder. But unexpectedly, she accepted the toastmaker but returned the JMG to me, saying until we were married, she would not accept such gifts from me. I asked her the reason for this and she said, "Manav, in case we do not get married, I want these items to be in your family." I was perplexed and asked, "But why? Why won't we get married? And why do you keep saying these things?" She did not reply and hung up. I was annoyed with her abrupt behaviour and decided not to talk to her. She kept calling me but I ignored her calls for a few days. It was the 20th of February when I heard a sudden knock on my door. I looked through the eyehole and found that it was Mansi. She was walking back and forth and looked very angry. I quickly filled two cups with the coffee I had been making and opened the door. She was standing there with her hair tied in a bun, and was looking at me with her stern eyes and folded hands. I kept looking at her and then, after a few seconds, broke into an unreasonable smile. She came closer and, looking into my eyes, asked, "Why didn't you take my calls?" I remained quiet for sometime and then, holding her hands, said, "Because you hung up that day without saying anything." She kept looking at me and then, holding me tight, said, "You don't understand why I said whatever I said. It's really tough for me to accept such gifts." I giggled a bit and then, kissing her on the forehead, said, "It's ok dear. I understand..." We kept holding each other for a few minutes and then sipped the lukewarm coffee, which had lost its hotness due to the delay. After we finished the coffee, we went for a long drive. It was the 20thof February and Mansi's birthday was on the 21st.

I wished Mansi exactly when the clock struck twelve. She saw my message and replied, "Thank you, Mr. Mad...Let's go to sleep." The next morning, I went to Mansi's colony and called her. She picked up my call and I requested her to come down. She was not yet ready and fumbled as she said, "Yeah...coming...coming...wait." I waited there for ten minutes after which I saw Mansi coming down wearing a white suit. As she came towards me, I wished her once again and gave her a red rose along with a small necklace. She took the rose, kissed it and kept it inside her purse. One of my friends, Nitesh, had planned to go along with me somewhere. I informed that to Mansi. She felt hurt and said, "Manav, on this day as well you don't have time for me." Then I realized my mistake and, feeling guilty, I decided to spend the entire day with Mansi. So we drove all the way to a nearby mall and then to the Kalkaji Mandir. On our way to the Wipro office, we stopped near a park and went for a walk. It was early in the morning and there was plenty of time on our hands. We held each other's hands and walked on the green grass. Our warm heels could feel the cool dew that had settled on the grass blades, and we talked about our personal worries. After walking for a while, I pulled Mansi closer and gently pecked her on her cheeks. She blushed and put her hands on my shoulders. Her beautiful eyes were gleaming in the sunlight and her sweet breath caressed my lips as she drew me in closer for a kiss. I held her in my arms and kissed her on her forehead. We kept holding each other for another few minutes and then continued on our journey. When we reached her office, we found that we were early that day and the janitor asked us to wait for a few minutes before he could open the gates. I asked Mansi to take out the necklace so that I could put it around her neck, but she said that she would prefer doing it somewhere else. So, we talked some more, after which Mansi waved me goodbye and went to work.

I was restless that day and roamed all over the NCR mall in search of something to buy for Mansi. I looked at some earrings and some jewellery, but none of it appealed to my taste. While returning from office, I showed Mansi the two tickets to the movie, Ghazini, which I had bought while she had been away at work. She jumped up with joy and said, "Oh I am so happy. We are going to watch a film together. Ahhh…" I smiled and replied, "This is the first time we are going for a movie together. It will be great…" She sweetly nodded her head and blew a few flying kisses.

Spice Mall was a place we often visited and spent quality time together. It was the nearest mall from Mansi's hostel, and thus became our favourite place to hang out. After spending a sleepless night, the next day, I got ready by 9 a.m. and left for Spice Mall. I reached the mall and waited outside a Haldiram's store on the ground floor. Fifteen minutes later, I saw her coming. My heart fluttered as she waved.

There was still an hour for the movie to begin, so we got busy trying out some clothes. Mansi had the innate skill of picking out different colours and patterns in clothes, and I just stood there, her only dumb companion. The browsing process was a prolonged one, and consisted of minute observation of various aspects of fashion and art. Although I appreciated art, I had the least amount of interest in spending time on clothes. I pulled Mansi out from the clothes section and urged her to visit some other sections as well.

Inside the theatre, we picked up a couple of colas and popcorns and settled on our seats. *Ghazini* is a Bollywood movie in which a business tycoon falls in love with a girl, and the two develop a very deep relationship and plan to get married. Everything goes fine until, one day, the girl is murdered by some dacoits and the guy is hit hard on his head by a rod. The latter develops a short-term memory disorder due to his injury, but the last whisper of his fiancée, mentioning the name of the killer, still reverberates in his ears. The movie portrayed tragedy and revenge in such a manner that it made us deeply emotional. While coming out of the theatre, Mansi was weeping. She was afraid that we might get separated one day due to inevitable reasons and thus succumb to our emotional deficiencies. But I held her close to me and reinforced the fact that I would never leave her under any condition. Seeing her sad always made me feel guilty; thus, to make the mood lighter, I gently pulled the tip of her nose and said, "Well, I don't know about you, but I am never gonna leave you." She suddenly looked up and, punching me right near my heart, said, "So that is what you think of me, huh? You are very bad. Get lost." I pulled her by her hands and said, "Where are you going, my mad girl? I said that I am never gonna leave you." Although we both were unsure about our future, we just kept enjoying our present moment. I held Mansi's hand and we walked down the stairs to the parking area. For the rest of the day, we drove to various places, had ice-cream, went to the Kalkaji Mandir, and clicked photographs. It was a great day spent with Mansi, and after having our dinner in a nearby restaurant, I dropped her at her hostel. That night, we were too tired to remain awake, and thus did not have the energy to talk further. Thus, we wished each other Good night and went to sleep.

My birthday was approaching in a few days, and I was unaware of Mansi's plans. She had designed and created a very beautiful birthday card for me. She had been preparing it over the last 10-12 days, but I had not been aware of it at all. On my birthday, she gifted me that card along with a beautiful watch.

Although I had had a minor fight with Mansi 2-3 days before my birthday, she managed to cool things down and celebrated my birthday in the most beautiful way possible.

Our relationship was growing exponentially. Mansi often complained that we were going too fast, and I could never comprehend what she actually meant by that. She said that Deepak and Neha went on a date after three years of their relationship, and that I had kissed her within just a few months after proposing. I listened to these things in utter amusement and then requested Mansi not to compare our relationship with others'. For me, our relationship was a unique one, and whenever she drew examples, I just lost my temper and often got infuriated by her words. Sometimes, we did quarrel over such trivial matters, but at the end of the day, everything just fell into place. Mansi had always wanted to come to my house, but I never got the right opportunity to welcome her. It was the month of November, and my birthday was drawing nearer. Mansi seemed to be very excited, and eventually, God graced Mansi with an opportunity to spend a day at my house. It was a Sunday, and my mom and brother had gone to our hometown for some urgent work. I made all possible arrangements to welcome her. It is in our custom to give a silver coin to a newly married bride or fiancée when she enters the house for the first time. Although we were not married, our relationship had become quite serious, and thus I bought a silver coin for Mansi.

Early in the morning, I woke up and went to pick her up from her place. I was excited as well as anxious. It would be her first time coming to my house, and I had to ensure everything was in proper order. I did not want her to form a lousy impression of me, and thus, I arranged things as best as I could. When Mansi came to my house, she was fascinated by the flowers in our small garden and appreciated the way in which they were being maintained. We both went inside, and I asked her to make herself at home while I made coffee. She went inside my room and started looking through some of my books. She was reading through one of them when I suddenly went and held her from behind. She was surprised and then broke into a delightful smile. She asked me for one of my shirts. I was amazed at this sudden, unexpected request, but gave her my black shirt. She wrapped herself in that like a small bird and then kissed it. I still have that shirt and have kept it like some valuable treasure.

Mansi said that she would really enjoy staying in my room as it was more comfortable than her hostel room. We talked for a few minutes and then sat on the bed. The coffee was quite warm, and we took turns sipping it from each other's cups. Time seemed to fly like wild horses and we were engaged in an endless conversation. I had never talked to anyone in my life for so long; our eyes were locked in each other, and we soon turned oblivious to the surroundings. Mansi held my hands and took me to the wall on which a calendar bearing the photo of God was hanging. We folded our hands and then prayed for a minute or two. Mansi came closer and hugged me tightly with a sigh of relief, and we kissed each other. After that day, there were a number of occasions when I managed to spend some time with Mansi at my house. We had many emotional moments; we spent a good amount of time together within the closed walls, but we never crossed our extreme limits. There were times when I felt scared, but I had full faith that nothing terrible would happen. One day, Mansi and I were talking about horoscopes; during college days, I used to check my horoscope and how it matched with Mansi's quite often. But unfortunately, we had no matching attributes in our horoscopes, and that was what bothered me the most. My anxiety was elevated further when Mansi said that her family members were very rigid regarding horoscopes, and would never agree for the marriage if they found any sort of anomaly.

Mansi had also got a call from the Indian Navy for joining in the Officer's cadre. Although she always dreamt of joining the defence forces, she let that proposal go because the post was a transferable one, and that could have seriously affected our relationship as I was working in an MNC in Delhi. But that was not so much of a relief since there were other problems along the way, the most immediate one being the horoscope matter.

I decided not to inform Mansi about the fact that our horoscopes didn't match, and thought of another way to resolve the issue. There was, and still is, an astrologer in Mandi, Himachal Pradesh—Dr. Lekhraj. I came to know about him through one of my friends, Veer. Dr. Lekhraj was a very good palmist, and I told him about my problem.

He laughed at first, and then advised me to bring Mansi along with me and told me not to worry too much. I told Mansi about the appointment fixed in Meerut, and she agreed to go along with me. We caught the earliest ride we could afford and reached Dr. Lekhraj's chamber. My heart was going pit-a-pat as we entered the room. Dr. Lekhraj looked at me, and in a rasping voice, welcomed me and Mansi. He was a retired Army officer and had a very good sense of humour. He saw Mansi's hand first and then my hand. After collecting some vital information regarding our horoscope, he said that we need not worry at all, and that our marriage was very much possible. He assured Mansi that there was absolutely no problem in marrying a Jain[21] boy like me, and that we would have two children after our marriage: first a baby boy and then a baby girl. All this might seem quite dramatic, but our marriage depended on this, and thus I requested Dr. Lekhraj to give me a printed copy of the result.

Mansi looked quite relieved after hearing everything, and assured me that everything was going to be perfect soon. After the appointment, we went to Gol market in Meerut—the place where Kartik and I used to go very often—and then we came back to Delhi. Everything went smoothly that day, and I somewhat started to believe that my world of fantasy was finally going to become a reality. I cannot say what I felt then; it was as if grey clouds had gathered above the dreary desert sand, promising heavy rainfall.

---

[21] Jainism, traditionally known as Jain Dharma, is an ancient Indian religion. Followers of Jainism are called "Jains", a word derived from the Sanskrit word jina (victor) referring to the path of victory in crossing over life's stream of rebirths by destroying karma through an ethical and spiritual life

For the next few days, I was so busy with my work that I hardly had time to properly talk to Mansi. She was busy too, and thus we could not have our heartfelt conversations any longer. I was sure that Mansi would call me, but she seldom did. I took her lack of response to be the result of workload, and thus did not disturb her unless there was a dire need. Although we had our daily conversations regarding our general health and well-being, we could not afford those late night chats any longer. One fine morning, as I was about to brush my teeth, my cell phone blared. It was Mansi!

"Hello miss, how are you?"

"I'm fine. What about you? Early today?"

"Yeah, just trying to catch up with my would-be-wife."

"Hmnn."

"What hmnn?? It's morning and not night."

"Yes. I wanted to tell you something important."

"Ooo. Really? What is it? Did you again do something which you should not have done? Hahaha..."

"It's not at all funny, Manav. Try to understand the gravity of the situation."

"Yeah. Let me brush my teeth first."

"How long will it take? Shall I call later?"

"No...No... Just say it."

"Ok! So the thing is that Mom called me today."

"Oh my God! This seems very serious. So did you tell her about me?"

"Ah! Wait. It's not about you."

"Hmnn. Keep going."

"So she said that she has selected a groom for me in Noida. And I have to go and meet him."

"What? Why?? No need."

"Ohoo. Just try to understand the thing. I have to go. Mom has told me."

"Did you tell her about me?"

"What? No I did not."

"Why not, miss?"

"I don't know. Why didn't you inform your parents about us, huh?"

"Alright...So what have you decided?"

"What do you mean by that?"

"I mean what are you going to do regarding this?"

"Of course I am going to reject him."

"Hmn. Ok, so shall I accompany you?"

"What! Are you mad? No way. I am going with my parents."

"Alright! I get it..."

"Don't worry. Everything is going to be fine."

"Hmn. I wish the same."

"Ok bye. I have to get ready now. Talk to you later sweetheart!"

"Yeah. Bye. Go safe and make sure you reject and come back fast."

"Hmn. Mad boy."

"And yes, let me know what all happened."

"Ok! May I go now?"

"Hmn!"

"Ok bye!"

"Yes, bye!"

You can well comprehend the kind of ill thoughts that traversed my mind throughout the entire day. I became restless and checked my cell phone after every ten minutes for any notifications. From the moment Mansi called, the world started turning topsy-turvy for me. I knew that I would have to face such situations in life, but I had never anticipated that these things would take place so soon. It was like a shock for me, and for the first time in my life, I cried for nearly thirty minutes. They say that one negative stroke is ten times more powerful than a positive stroke, and that is what I felt at that very moment. But I could not just sit and wait for Mansi's call, because earlier too, I had done that mistake, and I did not want to repeat it. Thus, I went to an astrologer I knew, and narrated the whole episode to him. He calmed me down and told me to do some things. I did all of them, but at the core of my heart, I still felt that things were going wrong. It was like an intuition that sparks up just before a storm.

After nearly 17 hours, Mansi called me:

"Hello... So how was your day?"

"It was fine. So what happened?"

"What would happen, mad boy? I went along with my mom and rejected the proposal. Simple!"

"Good. Do you know how worried I was?"

"Why were you worried? That means you do not trust me."

"No, it's not that. Actually, the problem is parents."

"Yes. Mom was angry with me today."

"Why?"

"Because I rejected the proposal."

"Why don't you tell her about me?"

"I don't know. My parents are orthodox, and probably will get infuriated by the news."

"But we have got to sort this out, Mansi. Tell me, don't you love me?"

"Yes, I do. But..."

"But what? Isn't love reason enough to confess about our relationship?"

"Yes. But I am afraid."

"What is there to be afraid of?"

"Tell me; have you told your parents about us?"

"No I haven't, but I will tell them soon."

"So, why haven't you told them till now? Please don't blame me."

"Who said that I am blaming you, dear?"

"No. I mean, you are acting as if I am the main culprit and as if I had decided to go and check out the groom."

"No. I never said that. I am just worried about our future."

"Making things turn out the way we want them to is not that easy, Manav! Please try to understand."

"But I believe that love can transcend boundaries and solve the hardest of problems."

"There is a difference between theory and practical life!"

"Ok. So, let's do it this way—I am going to go to your house tomorrow. Then your mom will understand the depth of our relationship."

"What?? No. I have to tell mom first."

"Whatever! I am going tomorrow. No further discussion."

"Ok... But remember that my parents are very much conservative. They might not like your coming to our house like this."

"We'll see to that. Ok. Bye for now..."

"Well then...Bye..."

After that, Mansi informed her mom that I would be coming to talk to her. At first, she was against it to due to family & cultural differences. Their rules did not allow their children to get married with an inter-caste boy. Her mother feared that society might boycott them, and she even told Mansi that there might be complications in her brother's marriage as well.

But after repeatedly insisting, she was a bit convinced and asked for my horoscope. Mansi had my horoscope with her and gave it to her Mom. Maybe she wanted to meet me at least so that she would be able to imagine the intensity of our relationship. Since I was a Jain boy, perhaps I got a spot among the top ranks on her community ranking ladder.

After getting the horoscope scrutinized by her trustworthy astrologer, she told Mansi that our horoscopes did not match at all, and that even if we got married, one of us would surely die after that. Hearing all this, I was depressed, but thought of talking to her mother regarding the horoscope case. Mansi gave me a green signal, and thereafter, I started all of my preparations. Just a day before leaving, I went to my brother-in-law to get some solid advice.

It was late in the evening when I met one of my brothers-in-law to inform him about my decision. He was a decent man, and I gained confidence after talking to him about Mansi and my relationship. He was the only one among our relatives who knew about this, and had promised to keep it a secret until everything got sorted out. When I reached his place, he was playing a game of pool. I requested him to give me some time and he immediately came with me to hear my problem. After hearing the entire matter, he patted on my shoulders and said that I needed to get ready for the big moment. Mansi's house was in Dehradun, and I had planned to drive all the way to her home. I was feeling nervous, but I had no choice. I had to know the actual problem. I wanted them to realise the fact that Mansi and I were more than friends. I wanted them to know how much I loved Mansi.

The next morning, I woke up early, took a long shower, wore my best outfit, combed my hair well and drove towards Mansi's house. A lot of confusing thoughts were flooding my mind as I began to prepare myself for the first encounter. I was, and still am, quite good with my communication skills. But there was a different type of fear that day which made me restrained. Moreover, I had heard that the parents of the girl whom you love generally tend to be a bit dramatic about the whole thing, and I was completely ready for all scenarios. All I wanted was to make a good impression.

It was around 1:00 p.m. when I reached her home. At the very first glance, it looked like an old house—ones which were made in the late '70s and '80s. The paint on the walls had peeled away, leaving behind spots at various places. The upper windows were unpainted and seemed as if they had been locked for years. But the surroundings were very well-maintained. As I proceeded, I first saw the garden filled with various types of plants. The leaves had covered half of the entrance from my view, and thus I had a very tough time finding my way through them. I texted Mansi regarding my arrival, and she said that her mom would escort me inside. In my utter desperation, I could not wait and somehow made my way inside. After sometime, I saw her grandmother, who was sitting on a chair and enjoying the morning sunshine. Her eyes gleamed as she looked at me with utmost curiosity. Just as I was about to interact with her, Mansi's mother arrived and I immediately touched her feet. Mansi's mother was as beautiful as Mansi. She had worn a reddish-brown sari and had combed her hair and tied it in a pony-tail. She welcomed me with a smile and then requested me to wait in the drawing room. The drawing room was neatly arranged with two sofas, a ceiling fan and beautiful pictures on the wall. Among the things which caught my attention were a few black-and-white family photographs and some artificial flowers. Mansi had told me that there used to be a time when her uncles and aunts stayed in the same house with them; after some family turmoil, they got separated and her father took charge of the house. As these things were tossing inside my mind, her mother came with a glass of water and sat just opposite to me on a wooden chair. She remained quiet for some time and then asked me about my journey from Delhi to Dehradun. Our conversation was just building up when her grandmother came inside and interrupted us by asking my identity. Her mother was smart in tackling these questions and immediately said that I was one of her relatives. You should have seen that old lady's face. She acted as if I was her family member and greeted me with the utmost reverence. So, the conversation went on for some time and then Mansi's mother went to the kitchen to prepare a cup of tea. When she came back, I started talking about Mansi. She was completely aware of the fact that I loved Mansi and treated me like a special friend of hers. She said in a tone of hesitation that her daughter, Mansi, never made male friends. Hearing this, I became sure that none of my endeavours were going to work and thus reverted to the previous topics of weather, pollution, and jobs. I eagerly wanted to bring up the main topic but somehow I could not do it for a long time. Finally, after an hour or two, I spoke to her mother about our relationship and said that I really loved her. The grandmother was shocked to hear this and said in Garhwali[22] that such things would never be accepted. Mansi's mother requested her not to interrupt and then asked me, "You are a very good guy. Any girl will want to marry you. Why then do you want to marry only our daughter?" I replied that I wanted to marry Mansi because I loved her and because I felt that she was the only one who

---

[22] Garhwali people are an Indo-Aryan ethno-linguistic group who primarily live in the Garhwal region of the Indian state of Uttarakhand and speak the Indo-Aryan Garhwali language. Any person who has ancestral Garhwali roots or lives in Garhwal and has a Garhwali heritage is called a Garhwali

would complete my life. Her mother smiled for a moment and then said that love is quite complex and blind. She said, "By the way, your horoscopes do not match. See Manav, the same thing happened in my family too. My sister married the man with whom she had horoscope problems. Just a year after their marriage, her husband died. I don't want this to repeat for my own daughter." I quickly took out the horoscope reports developed by Dr. Lekhraj and handed them over to her. She looked through them minutely, and I even asked her to get them checked by her trusted astrologer. After a couple of minutes, I stood up and took her permission to leave. She escorted me till the gate and then I drove home safely.

When I reached home, I told Mansi all that had happened and she kept laughing. I asked her about the poor condition of her house and she said that the house would be renovated soon. I wanted to know her mother's reactions after I left, but Mansi said that she had not appeared in front of her mother. After talking for a few hours, I apologised to Mansi and admitted that it had really been very hard to admit the actual thing to her mother. She kept laughing like a fool and said, "Well then... Finally, you understood my problem." We both laughed for a few seconds and then silence prevailed. I was tired from the long day's journey and thus wished Mansi a sweet 'Good night' and went to sleep.

There was a Jain temple in Hastinapur[23], near Meerut. I had a lot of faith in that place. It had some sort of a positive power that could heal any problem in life. Although people with sound logic might call it a case of the placebo effect, I believed in that place, and seeing all things going wrong,

---

[23] City in the province of Uttar Pradesh

wanted to take Mansi there. So off we went to Hastinapur and returned after 4-5hours. Mansi and I believed that everything would soon turn out to be perfect, and with that thought in our minds, I dropped Mansi at her paying guest and went home.

After a few days, Mansi asked me to go to Vaishno Devi in Himachal Pradesh. Mansi had huge faith in the shrine of the Devi temple in Vaishno Devi, and so we decided to go there as well. I booked the tickets from Delhi, and we reached there at around 11 a.m. next day. We searched for a decent hotel there, and after getting refreshed, started our journey to the main temple situated at the top of the mountain. All the way up, Mansi held my hands tight, and we were praying to God to resolve our issues. It was nearly dusk by the time we reached the top, and after crossing the long tunnel, we entered the main holy temple. There was a priest standing over there, and Mansi gave her mom's red scarf as a devotional offering to the goddess. After doing his prayer and saying his *mantras*[24], he returned it to us with some sweets as *prasad*[25].

After completing our journey, we came back to the hotel, stayed there, and took a short nap of 4-5 hours. Then we woke up, packed our things, and returned to Delhi.

---

[24] A mantra is usually any repeated word or phrase, but it can also refer more specifically to a word repeated in meditation. Mantra comes from a Sanskrit word meaning a "sacred message or text, charm, spell, counsel
[25] Prasad (also called prasada or prasadam) is a material substance of food that is a religious offering in both Hinduism and Sikhism. It is normally consumed by worshippers. 'Prasad' literally means a gracious gift

Deadlock

Do you remember the night when Mansi called me and said that she had done something with someone at Iqor? Well, she often played such pranks on me which made me go crazy. And most importantly, these types of pranks were the root cause of our quarrels. Well, I would not say that it was always that way, but yeah, most of the time, it was that way. Another similar incident happened that night; we were busy chatting at around 11:30 p.m. when suddenly, Mansi said that she was having a headache. I was worried about her, but also wondered whether it was a prank. She said, "Do something Manav, my head is paining a lot." I took it lightly and said, "Oh My God... What will I do now? It is already 11:45 p.m. and I can't go out of my house... Wait, let me contact someone." Mansi got very much annoyed with this and said, "What?? So this is how much you love me? Wao..."

"Tell me, what can I do? It's already very late. Try and understand."

"Fine! No need to do anything for me."

"No... Wait. I have asked Neeraj to bring some medicines for you."

"What? Neeraj? Why?? I don't need the meds."

"Hey, but why?"

"When I need you, you are not here. It's better that I marry Neeraj then!"

She went offline after saying this, and I became frustrated by the situation. After a few minutes, Neeraj called and informed me that Mansi had told him not to bring the medicines for her. I was really upset with this news. Moreover, I could not understand how Mansi had Neeraj's number. So I called Neeraj and asked him whether he had shared his number with Mansi or not. He said that Mansi had once asked for his number so that she might contact him in case of any need. I became furious with this and called Mansi. I waited till four rings but she did not pick it up. The next morning, I called her and asked her the reason for keeping Neeraj's number with her. She got agitated by my question and asked me the reason for being nosy. I lost control over myself and hung up the phone in utter disgust.

At this point of my life, I was working for Nagarro Softwares, a technical consultancy company. Our main job was to fix mistakes in our clients' systems and software. All my friends were working in reputed companies with handsome salaries, and thus I wanted to elevate my position as well. Life was getting tougher day by day, and under immense workload, I almost lost all the happiness of my life. Mansi used to call me whenever she got free and kept informing me about the various groom offers that were piling up at her house. I was so busy that I could not find time to sort things out in a better way. It was not that I was ignorant to this pressing issue of groom offers, but I was in a helpless situation and expected Mansi to help me. I felt like I was lost in the middle of the sea, and thus got busy finding my career path.

One morning, Mansi called me and asked me to meet her at a park near her hostel in the evening. There was a bit of numbness in her voice and I could immediately sense that something was wrong. Before I could ask her anything regarding this, she cut the call. I had to go to my office and thus did not call her back. I was afraid that it was something regarding the groom offers and her mother. Although I went to office, I could not focus on any task. The last call of Mansi kept floating in my mind and I was just waiting for the hours to fly past as soon as they could. When it was around six o'clock in the evening, I left the office and went to meet Mansi. She was standing near the entrance of the park. She had tied her hair into a pony-tail and was wearing an orange jumpsuit. I smiled at her as she approached me. We both went inside and talked about various things regarding our jobs. I told her about my hectic schedule and also informed her that by the next month, I was going to be promoted to a very high post in the company. Mansi heard all I had to say and then congratulated me. I was so excited to meet Mansi after so many days that I almost forgot about her phone call. After talking for some time, Mansi asked me to sit on one of the benches and then said, "See Manav, I have to tell you something very important." I knew that from the very beginning of the day! Suppressing my anxiety, I asked her to speak further. She said, "My parents are obsessed with my marriage, and a lot of groom offers are coming in our house. I tried to explain to my parents about you and they said that you have time till the 31st of May." I was taken aback and asked whether her mother said something about me or not. She remained ignorant to that question and reinforced the fact that her parents were very serious regarding the matter. I told her not to worry and then, as I was about to place my hand on her shoulders, she moved away. This made me angry and I said, "What's wrong with you?"

"Nothing."

"So why are you acting abnormal today?"

"You simply do not have time for me. That night, I suffered a lot. You did not come."

"Oh come on, Mansi! You know that it was very late that night and it was practically impossible for me to step out of my house."

"Alright, so have you informed your parents regarding our relationship?"

"No. But I will inform them very soon."

"Soon?? What soon? You have time till the 31st of May only. After that, if I marry someone else, then please don't accuse me for anything."

"What? So that is what it boils down to? That is the price you pay for love?"

"Well, then please go ahead and inform your parents right away. Please don't create a scene here."

"Scene? What scene? This is getting serious."

"Yes, that is what I just said. Things are getting worse day by day." Saying this, she stood up and walked away. She did not even turn around and look at me. I had never expected Mansi to leave me in such a situation. I admit that I could not build up the courage to confess to my parents... Even Mansi helped me by giving sufficient time. I had suggested many a time that we could opt for a court marriage, but she refused completely. I was aware that if we got married once, then our parents would have to somehow accept the matter. But Mansi was adamant about her decision. I was between the devil and the deep sea, and started thinking of plans to introduce Mansi to my family members.

My family members were not that conservative, but I did not want to introduce Mansi to them just like that. Fortunately, my brother's marriage was fixed on March of that year and I saw it as a clear opportunity to introduce Mansi to my family members. So, as the marriage day drew closer, I invited all of my friends and called Mansi to inform about the ceremony. I kept calling her but she did not pick up. Everyone in the house was very busy, and I had to help my mother in preparing some items that were essential for the marriage ceremony. Thus, I did not have the time to text her at that very moment. However, when I came back to check my phone after a few hours, I was quite shocked to see that there was no response from her side. I got very angry with her aloofness and thus decided not to invite her. Although I had decided not to call her again, I did text her and inform her about the ceremony. She saw the messages but did not reply. Feeling depressed, I thought of refreshing my mood a bit and thus went ahead to enjoy with my family and friends in the marriage party. Due to some problems from the bride's side, the atmosphere in my home was not good, and I thought that it would be best to introduce Mansi to my family separately. Things had taken a turn for the wrong in my family only recently, and bringing up the topic of Mansi would only do more harm than good.

It was all going wrong! Although I enjoyed in my brother's marriage, I could not get over the constant fear and psychological agony that bugged my optimistic mind and made me get angry over trivial matters. Moreover, it was not just me; my family was falling apart too. My father had a big altercation with my uncle regarding the family business, and my uncle decided to split ways with us. This worsened matters and further decreased my chances of introducing Mansi to my parents. She had given me time till the 31st of May, but I needed more time. Hence, to inform her about my problems, I called her up at around 7:30 in the evening. I kept calling her but she did not pick up. I got frustrated and thought of going to her hostel to enquire about the situation. I called her 98 times but she did not pick up even once. At first, the thought that something bad had happened to Mansi troubled me. But after that, I saw that she had been online just a couple of minutes ago, and this infuriated me to the highest limits. That night, at the dinner table, I accidentally broke a glass of water and did not eat properly. After finishing all her tasks, my mother came and sat beside me. She placed one hand on my head and asked, "What is the matter, Manav? You don't look well." When she asked me this, I thought of telling her everything. But I thought of the family condition and the pressures my parents were facing, and ultimately replied that I was just fine. My mother spent some time with me and then left. I could not sleep properly that night and kept thinking about what I was to do next. I check my phone but there were no notifications. Just as I was about to switch it off, Mansi called me. Although I did not want to pick up her call, I did.

"How are you Manav?"

"Not well. And I don't want to talk to you anymore. What do you think, huh? That you will keep behaving like this with me and I will keep suffering?"

"Please listen to me for a moment."

"Yes, yes... What more should I listen to? Those silly groom offers! That's what this is about, right?"

"No. It's something different."

"Whatever! I don't want to listen. Do you even see the number of times I called you?"

"I saw. 98 times. I was outside, so could not pick up."

"Ooo, another groom appointment?"

"No. I went shopping with my mother."

"Good! Stay there."

"Come on. Don't be mean."

"Yes. Now I am being mean. Do you even know how much I love you? Do you know how worried I was?"

"Alright, all I wanted to ask you was whether you would be able to come and meet me at Noida tomorrow or not."

"Where in Noida?"

"I am sending you the address through a message."

"Alright. But when?"

"At around 11:00 in the morning."

"Alright, I shall be there. Hey! Is this about something important?"

"I don't hope so."

"So what is it that you are going to tell me tomorrow?"

"For that you have to wait till tomorrow."

"I can't; please tell me. At least tell me what this is about."

"It's nothing. I just want to meet you."

"No. I sense something is wrong. Please tell me what it is."

"Hey, I have to go now. See you tomorrow."

"Hey wait."

"Can't. Mom is calling me."

"Alright, take care, and yes Good night."

"Yup, Good night."

"I love you."

"Hmn. Bye..."

"Buh-bye!"

Although Mansi had said that there was nothing serious, I strongly felt that something was wrong. I believed that Mansi and I could make things work out at last. It is said that when you really think in a positive way, good things happen to you. Thus, the next morning, I went to the guest house in Noida where Mansi had asked me to come and waited for her. I called Mansi and she said that she would be there within ten minutes. She arrived, took my hands in hers, and said, "Come. Let's go to the nearby temple." But I was not willing to go anywhere and hence I said, "No, we are not going anywhere today. We are going to talk and enjoy today." She seemed a bit nervous and said, "I would go to the temple first." She was practically right. Our relationship had suffered a lot of setbacks and thus, I thought that going to the temple to seek the blessings of the lord would be a good idea. We went to the nearby temple, removed our shoes at the entrance, and stepped inside. The whole temple was divided into three smaller sections. First, we went and prayed in front of Lord Krishna, then we went to the shrine of Lord Rama and Sita. Finally, we visited the last shrine of Lord Shiva. Mansi stood there for a long time, praying. When she opened her eyes after praying, I asked in a humorous tone, "What were you praying for so long huh, Mansi? For a good husband or what? Haha!" She got a bit annoyed and said, "Shut up, you mad boy!" I was elated, and to carry on the conversation, said, "Haha! Don't worry; I am a very good guy." Mansi burst into laughter and said, "Yes...yes...Of course." We both held each other's hands and strolled inside the temple. Opposite to Lord Shiva, there was an idol of Vaishno Devi. I looked at it and said to Mansi, "Accha Mansi, what if our parents do not allow us to marry?"

"Well, then I don't know. I guess they won't tell such things."

"Hmn. But what if they do, Mansi?"

"I don't know. You tell me..."

"Well, that is a very tough question I see. We would run away and marry..."

"What?? Run away and marry? Never. I would never ever do that."

"Why Mansi, don't you love me?"

"Being in love and fleeing to marry are completely different prospects."

"Well, then we would never marry, but stay together."

"What? No, that would not be possible because if you don't marry me, then there would be no order in our relationship and you might leave me someday."

"I am never going to leave you, miss."

"Hmn, time shall say."

"Do you have faith in me?"

"I have, but time is very less, Manav."

"See Mansi, I need a bit more time. Things in our family are not going well. Uncle just separated from us, and the condition of our family is very bad now."

"So do you think that things in our family are going good?"

"No, I mean I just need more time..."

"See, I don't know about all this. I requested you to introduce me to your parents but you did not. You did not even tell me about your brother's marriage beforehand."

"Yes, I admit that it was my fault, but please try to understand... Time heals almost everything."

"Maybe it does. But things are really getting worse day by day."

"Yes, I totally get it. I will introduce you to my parents after a few months."

"Why are you so scared? You said that your parents are really good and that they would talk to my parents..."

"Yes, they will talk to your parents. But situations have turned so sour that making any quick move now is quite impossible for me."

"And yes, by the way, you don't even care for me. That night I had such a bad headache and you did not even think of it as a priority."

"Come on, Mansi... Why are you still stuck in such trivial matters?"

"Wao! So my headache is a trivial matter for you."

"Oh! Please... For God's sake, try to understand."

Mansi held my hands and took me outside. She placed her hand on my chest and said, "I love you, but I guess you don't." I was astonished to hear this, and retorted saying that I loved her more than she could ever imagine. Mansi looked into my eyes and then said, "We must go home now." I came closer to Mansi and said, "Don't worry, *jaanu*. Everything will be fine. Try and talk to your parents and give me a bit more time. We will fix everything." She nodded her head and then turned to walk away from me. I said, "I love you, Mansi. I love you a lot." Hearing this, she stopped and turned back. I could see her face clearly. She smiled a bit and then said, "Make sure you go home safely...and yes...we will make things work. Don't worry..."

Things were starting to get complicated. The time extension till 31st of May 2012, which I had somehow managed from Mansi, had long passed. It was the first day of January in the year 2013 when Mansi called me and threatened to break the relationship. It was the date when our relationship had begun, and I wanted to spend that day with her. But she sent me some sort of an absurd message thanking me for all that I had done for her. I was quite astonished to see this as I had not done everything for her for gaining something. I helped her and supported her only because I loved her a lot. I immediately called one of my friends, Deepak, and fixed a plan to meet at a mall in Noida. Mansi and her sister came to the mall, and we sat down to talk regarding our relationship. Deepak and I tried to convince Mansi that I would surely introduce her to my family members as soon as possible. But not a word could move her adamant mind. She got up from her seat and, walking away from me, said, "You have only one week…"

After two days, Mansi called me and asked me come to her hostel. After that, we went to the temple and sat there for some time. There was a tinge of sadness on her face which I could not comprehend. She had somehow turned more mysterious than before, and day by day, she was turning into someone whom I couldn't recognize.

After a few days, I heard that Mansi had left Noida and gone back to her hometown. Things were very difficult for me. My grandfather had succumbed to his illness and had passed away just then, and my family members were severely tormented by his departure. It was not like I did not want to introduce Mansi to my family members, but situations had suddenly turned so sour that I could not find the perfect moment to disclose my relationship. Things got aggravated when Mansi stopped replying and picking up my calls. I asked her many a time to go for a court marriage so that our family members would eventually agree to our relationship. But she never wanted to do anything without the consent of our parents. I had expected things to get tough with time, but had never imagined that things would get so tough. After all, love marriage, being a taboo in India, is still quite synonymous with hurdles. If there is no hurdle in the whole process, then it can surely be concluded that it is an arranged marriage and not a love marriage. But to pull through this situation, both of us needed to help each other. After all, marriage is a mutual thing, and cannot be accomplished alone. But I felt like I was the only one who was striving to keep the bridge between us during this storm. I called Mansi several times, and after a lot of trials, when she finally picked up, I asked her about her health and also told her about my present condition and requested her to cooperate with me for at least a month. But, on the contrary, she requested me not to narrate to her my doleful story. I was shocked to hear this and wanted an explanation for such a request. She remained silent for some time and then disconnected the call.

When I called back, I found her phone switched off! Things were all going wrong. I had heard somewhere that one should never ever trust any girl or woman because she could change anytime and anywhere. Hearing Mansi's reply, I had started to feel something of that sort.

Days passed in great depression, and suddenly one evening, Mansi called me. I took the call but remained silent. She said, "Hey, do not worry. Everything is alright. You do not have to tell anything to your parents about me…" This statement really gave me a bit of hope and I said, "How are you? Hey, don't worry, I am looking for the perfect moment to introduce you to my family…" Her voice had some sort of a detached feel to it and she replied, "Hey, if I marry someone else, will you come to my wedding ceremony?"

"Well, that was a very bad joke."

"Just tell me Manav, will you come?"

"Hahaha! Yes, of course. I shall come and then take you along with me."

"Come on, Manav, tell me seriously."

"What's wrong with you, huh? I admit that things are tough now, but we have to hold on to our hope...You just can't be like this, Mansi..."

"Don't teach me how I should be...just answer."

"Well, if that ever happens, then please do not inform me about it because I will not let anything of that sort to take place..."

After this, I hung up out of utter frustration and anger, and switched off the phone.

A Mistake to Be Proud Of

It was the 24th of July, and the last time I had talked to Mansi was three weeks ago. She had said that her family had received a groom offer from Dehradun—a boy who lived and worked outside India. We both had talked about it and I had had a bit of a quarrel with Mansi that day. She had said that she would go back to her home for a month or two, and thus I decided not to disturb her. I wanted to give her some space so that she could get a bit refreshed. Moreover, I had been promoted to a higher position in the company, which meant that now I had more responsibility and more workload. But on the 24th of July, I felt like having a nice evening chat with Mansi, and thus called her home's landline number. I was not afraid to confront her mom anymore, and wanted her parents to know that Mansi was a very special person for me. The phone kept ringing but there was no answer from the other end. After trying for nearly seven times, an unknown male voice replied from the other side:

"Hello! Who is this?"

"Yes...hello. I wanted to talk to Asha aunty. Is she there? I am Manav."

"Oh! But she has gone to her hometown for some work. I am their tenant."

"Can you tell me where she has gone?"

"No. I don't know anything regarding that."

In our last call, Mansi had told me that there was some traditional pooja at her village and so her mom and dad would go there. But still, I wanted to confirm the fact and thus asked, "Do you know what the work is?"

"They did not tell clearly, but it is regarding the marriage of their daughter I guess."

I was flabbergasted on hearing this, and could not believe my ears. I stammered while I asked, "Whose marriage?"

"Their daughter, Mansi..."

My arms and legs went numb. Beads of perspiration formed all over my forehead and I could not figure out what to do. It was like a thousand-volt shock for me. I quickly picked up my phone and called Neha. I called her seven times but she did not pick up the call. With each passing minute, my frustration grew exponentially. It was like someone had stabbed me right in my heart. I then called Mansi's elder sister, Surbhi. She picked up the call and said, "Yes, Akhilesh...Hi!"

She could not recognize that I was Manav because she had never talked to me over phone, and thus asked, "How is Mansi? I guess she was the one who told you to call me, right?" I did not want to prolong this any further and thus clarified that I was not Akhilesh but Manav. The moment she heard my name, she turned indifferent and replied, "Ohh...yes, Manav!"

"Yes didi. Mansi's number was not reachable so I called you. I heard that Mansi is going to get married. Is it true?"

"Yes Manav, she is going to get married within six months."

Although I could sense that she was framing the time-span of six months, I gently replied, "But she had told me that there is some pooja at your village."

"No Manav. She has not gone to the village. And yes, one more thing Manav, in our caste, we do not go for intercaste marriages."

I wasn't interested in whatever she had to say, and thus calmly replied that I would talk to her later and disconnected the call. This was sheer madness. By now, it was very clear that something was absolutely wrong. But I did not know whom to call for help. It was a very awkward situation, and all I had was a name—Akhilesh. I thought for a moment and then opened my Facebook account and started searching for the name in the friends list of Shweta, Sekhar, Surbhi, and all others I could think of. After browsing for about an hour, I found the profile of Akhilesh, an employee in Wipro Ltd. United States. I scrolled through his posts to see if someone had congratulated him or not. The thought that Mansi had already gotten married to this guy was playing at the back of my mind, and I was 90 percent sure of this fact. Mansi's parents had already been searching for someone outside India, and most importantly, both Akhilesh and Mansi were Garhwali. I was going through Akhilesh's friends on Facebook when I discovered that one of his brothers was studying in ICAI and was preparing for CA exams. I immediately dropped him a message:

"Hi, I was impressed by your profile. I am preparing for the CA exams too. I shall be highly obliged if you could guide me or give me your phone number so that I could contact you." Eventually, he shared his phone number with me and I called him, pretending to be Akhilesh's friend:

"Hello! Who's this?"

"Hi! I am Mayank, Akhilesh's friend from Bangalore."

"Yes Bhaiya. How are you?"

"I am quite well. How are you doing?"

"I am well too."

"Hey, I am trying to reach Akhilesh at his old number but it is showing that the number is invalid. Do you have his new number?"

"Yes, one minute. I am giving you the number."

"And by the way, I heard Akhilesh got married... Is this true?"

"Yes Bhaiya, elder brother got married on the 11th of July."

"Wao! And he did not even bother to invite me!"

"Haha! But a lot of his friends were invited."

"Wait...you just give me his number. I will talk to him"

"Haha...yes...I am texting you his number."

"Thank you very much! It was nice talking to you."

"My pleasure, Bhaiya."

By now, I was completely sure that Mansi had gotten married to Akhilesh, and I guess you can well comprehend the state of my mind and emotions. I was completely shattered. I called my brother-in-law and described the whole thing to him. He told me not to take any wrong steps in haste and told me that he was on his way to my house. I could not understand what had just happened and was completely dumb-founded. I was at my wit's end and saw all of my sweet dreams crumbling under the weight of unexpected reality. After some time, I called Mansi again.

She did not pick up the call at first, but I kept calling her again and again. Finally, she picked.

"Hey, how are you?"

"Oh Manav...I am fine. What about you?"

"I guess you know how I am. So the call was really serious, huh?"

"What? I didn't get you..."

"OK. Whatever. So how are your marriage plans coming along?"

"Yeah...There are two potential grooms whose profiles my parents want me to go through."

"Ooh...What do you mean by go through?"

"I mean, go for an appointment."

"Did you tell them about me? I mean, did you tell your parents regarding our marriage?"

"Yes...But time is very less."

"Ok! So what are the names of those 'two potential candidates' and where do they work?"

"One of them works in TCS, and the other is in some government bank. That's all I know, and I am not going to disclose their names to you."

"Ooh! Why won't you disclose their names to me? Don't you love me?"

"Actually, keeping their names a secret is sort of protocol for me."

"Wao...You are such an honest and truthful girl..."

"What do you mean by that?"

"No... Actually your brother called me today..."

"What brother? I don't have any brother."

"Oh...but he said that his name was some Akhilesh Bagarhwal. Perhaps he is a liar then..."

"What? How did you come to know this name?"

"Come on, please! Stop this drama with me, alright? I know everything, you liar! You have already married this guy whose name is Akhilesh Bagarhwal. He is an employee in Wipro and works in the United States. Just have some shame, Mansi...have some shame..."

She remained silent and I felt like murdering her at that very moment. She had played with me and my feelings and my time and my mind. And now, everything was a mess. I said, "Come on you liar. Tell me, why did you do this tome, huh? Just answer me...Oh, sorry...I forgot...Your stock of lies has been exhausted, right? What lie are you going to tell me now, huh?" Predictably, she remained silent. Minutes passed by, and after some time, I wished her all the best for her marriage and hung up.

Although I was strongly against alcohol consumption, and entire college was aware about it, that day, I mean... yes...that day, first and last time in my life, I walked into a bar and drank till late at night. Tears were streaming down my cheeks. It was as if the dam of my emotions had been broken, as if the vessel of my feelings had been wrecked. I was trying to drink away my pain. I still remember how I had lied to my parents that night. I told them that one of my friends had met with an accident and that I was with him. The friction of my life had suddenly increased, and my vehicle, filling with pain and agony, was quickly evaporating like vapours oozing from a water surface.

The next day, I called Mansi up but she did not pick up. I thought that she did not have her phone on her then, and thus called her home's landline number. After a few rings, someone with a cracking voice picked up the call and, out of disgust, I immediately hung up. I threw my phone away and went to take a nap. Just then, my phone rang. It was Mansi. I took the call:

"Hello betrayer, how are you?"

She started yelling at me in a harsh voice and said, "Listen carefully. I gave you enough time...It was your fault."

"Oh please! Don't give me this stupid reason. What do you mean by, gave me time? Is this some sort of selection exam or what?"

"Why did you call my home's landline number?"

"Because you were not picking up my calls."

"You cannot call like that...There are guests in the house."

"Oh! Guests...Yes, yes I forgot... You are married now."

"Please stop disturbing me, Manav."

"You should have said this to me a long time ago..."

"See, there are guests in the room and I have to go."

"Hmn. Tomorrow, I am coming to your house in Dehradun and then we shall have a nice talk. Just wait...I have a lot of things to tell your mom."

"Manav, Mom knows everything."

"Oh! Yes, I forgot. After all, she is your mother. The mother of a shameless liar must be like her daughter only..."

"Mind your language, Manav."

"Ok, whatever! I am coming tomorrow. I have a lot of things to say to Mr. Akhilesh."

I hung up and started preparing to leave for Dehradun. Mansi kept calling me, but I switched off the phone. Tears kept rolling down from my eyes and I collapsed on my bed. Memories from the past kept flashing on my mind, and I eventually cancelled my trip to Dehradun. There was a lot of pent up aggression, but in reality, I did not want to ruin her life. Moreover, Mansi had asked her mother to request me not to come, and after hearing this, I felt like burning her alive.

The next day, I called her and she picked up instantly.

"Please don't come..."

"Why did you do this to me?"

"Whatever I did, I did for the happiness of us both and that of our parents."

"You did not think about me for even an instant?"

"I had no other option..."

"That means you never loved me. All that you did was for your own benefit and for your parents."

"See, I want to meet you once before leaving to the U.S. I am not going without meeting you once. I told Akhilesh as well, and he said that we can all meet. So, I am planning to meet somewhere in Delhi."

"Alright...Have a nice life and always stay happy. That is all I want."

"Thank you very much...but do you really want me to bring Akhilesh along?"

"Yes...because I am not coming anywhere without him coming along."

"Alright. Let's not meet in Delhi then. I am going to Dehradun tomorrow, and I shall wait for both of you there."

"Ok..."

"Ok, bye for now."

"Bye!"

Hanging up, I immediately went out to buy some gifts for both of them. After pondering for a long time over various items, I bought a Zodiac shirt for Akhilesh and packed that juicer-mixer-grinder for Mansi, which I had kept at my home very carefully all this while.

The next morning, I left for Dehradun and took one of my friends along with me. On the way, I told him the whole story of how Mansi and I had met and all that had happened between us. He was quite sad after hearing everything and exclaimed that a needless drama had been played with me. When we were about to reach Dehradun, I called Mansi.

"Hey! We are about to reach Dehradun. So where shall we meet?"

"See, we have to visit our uncles too, and thus we don't have much time. So how about meeting in some restaurant at the railway station itself?"

I got angry and said, "Look! We have come a long way

from Delhi to meet you guys. Now if you don't have time for us then we can go back to Delhi. But if you want to meet me, then we shall meet at a proper place."

"Alright...first let me meet you at the railway station then we can decide where to go from there."

"Alright...we will be there in another seven minutes."

"Ok bye!'

When we stepped on the platform, we found ourselves in the midst of a huge crowd. It was impossible to recognize anyone properly. Suddenly, I heard someone calling my name from behind. I turned around and found Mansi standing there in her bridal dress, looking like an angel. Her eyes and her visage evoked all those memories once again in my mind—all those late-night chats, bike-rides, stupid jokes...everything flashed before my eyes and made me feel depressed. However, I took a deep breath and walked forward to greet them. Mansi said to Akhilesh, "Look...He is Manav."

I boldly walked forward and shook my hands with him. After talking to him for some time, I congratulated both of them and handed over their gifts to them. When I shook my hands with Mansi, I did not know how to react and thus kept it genuine with a sweet smile.

Akhilesh suggested that we go to a nearby restaurant, and we willingly agreed. I was curious about Akhilesh and got into a smooth conversation with him regarding his life in America and his work there. Mansi and my friend were coming behind us; I saw Mansi inspecting the wrapped box minutely and then, after a few minutes, she asked my friend,

"Is this a JMG?" My friend smiled a bit and then slowly nodded his head to indicate a "yes." Mansi looked at me and, for the first time in my life, I winked at her with a smile.

When we went to the restaurant, I sarcastically asked Akhilesh, "So why did not you invite us to your marriage?" Ina tone of regret, he said, "You should ask Mansi that...I told her to invite all her friends. I really don't understand why she did not invite you." Hearing this, I laughed, suppressing all the scars on my heart...

There was a pen which I had never lent anyone to use because I had kept it aside for Mansi. It is said that a pen is mightier than a sword, and thus I had wanted to gift a sword to Mansi as a symbol of strength, so that she might fight all her problems in life with confidence. But I finally took out the pen from my pocket and gave it to Akhilesh. After we finished our conversations, we took some photographs and then they left. My friend and I stayed there for a few more hours and ate a lot of delicious food. We took a nice tour of Dehradun and then, when it started getting dark, we booked tickets for the next train and left for Delhi.

Slowly, as the days passed by, I came to know that her mother had known almost everything regarding our affair. Although Mansi had left for the U.S., I stayed in touch with her mother, but never talked to her in a cordial way. Things had obviously changed a lot through the months, and I remember one certain incidence when her mother called me and I asked her the reason for playing with my emotions in spite of knowing everything regarding our relationship. She predictably dodged me without giving a proper reply, and I could not bear her silence any longer. Each and everything made me frustrated through these days, and I was completely in the clasp of anxiety.

One morning, her mother suddenly called me and said, "Mansi is coming here after a few days. She is going to stay here for a month and Akhilesh is going to go back after a few days. If you want to meet her during this time, you can." This news was like a raindrop on the desert sand of my broken heart. Moreover, I no longer took the words of these people seriously because I had seen their true colours and then had come to know that they were totally fake. However, hearing that Mansi was coming back to her hometown, I went out to buy a small gift for her which would always be there in front of her eyes and would remind her of me. It was really hard for me to believe that Mansi was no longer in my life. Even though we never spent time together, it was always soothing to know that there was at least someone with whom I could share all my thoughts without any restrictions. So, I was searching for something abstract but also relevant to gift Mansi. After juggling through a lot of things, I thought of buying a photo-frame from Archies, with which I would be able to make a collage and gift it to Mansi. It felt appropriate, as a photo-frame is the only thing that could always stay in front of her, and the photos in the collage would evoke our memories in her mind. My intention was not to remind her of our relationship, but to gift her something that I considered precious, and they were the memories that I had made with Mansi.

So, I reached her hometown, Rudraprayag, and informed her of my arrival over the phone. She said that she would meet me at the nearby Cafe Coffee Day and told me to wait there until she came. I waited for another fifteen minutes and then Mansi arrived. We went inside the cafe and took a corner seat. I kept silent and this time, Mansi started the conversation:

"So how was your journey from Delhi?"

"Awful. Nothing is going good. Why did you do this tome? Why?"

"It was our destiny, Manav."

"What destiny, huh? Please tell me what was the problem. Was there any spot on my character? Was I not settled?"

"It's nothing like that."

"So, am I not that handsome? Or did you leave me because I do not have a job in the States like an NRI?"

"See Manav, whatever has happened, has happened for the good of both of us."

"What good? Tell me, what good? I am dying out here without you. You could have clearly told me that you do not love me. Why did you do all that drama, huh?"

"See, you are not of our caste."

"You should have seen to that earlier. You knew very well that I would not be able to marry any other girl; still, you were okay doing this tome?"

"See Manav, get married and have a family. Everything will be okay."

"Oh please! Stop lecturing me about what I should do and what I should not. I can look after myself. But how could you do this, Mansi? How could you? I loved you so much. So this is the price of love, huh? Oh God, I loved you so much. No, my biggest mistake in the life was to love you, and now I am totally depressed. I feel like someone has left me alone in the middle of an ocean."

Tears started running down my cheeks and Mansi hung her head. She did not have the guts to look directly into my eyes. I felt like leaving that place immediately, but I stayed there. After sometime, one of the waiters came and asked us what we wanted to order. I ordered two coffees, which later had to be revised to only one since Mansi refused to eat anything because of her ill health. She remained silent and thus, to break the ice, I started the conversation this time:

"Ok...whatever...so how is life in U.S.A.?"

Mansi was sobbing and I felt great pain as I had to see her tears but could not do anything. I offered her a tissue paper, but she refused to take it from my hands and picked up another piece from the table. I requested Mansi to stop crying; but she could not control herself. To calm her and to break the tension of the situation,, I cleared my throat and said, "When you have your first child, I will send you a poem. After all, I am a close friend to you at least, am I not?" She stood up, pushed her chair away and then turned around to walk away. I said, "Wait, please. At least today... don't leave me today at least..." But she did not wait for me. She said, "I have to go and start packing for my return trip. I am happy, Manav... Make your own life. I was quite lucky to have you in my life. But..." I could not understand a bit of what she was saying. I asked, "But what? Please tell me the rest. Please..." But she did not wait any further and walked out of the cafe without wishing me goodbye or even turning back to look at me again. I asked Mansi about her date of departure and she said that she would leave India in mid-September. As I hardly believed her, I called her mother to confirm the same. But even she said that Mansi would leave in mid-September. However, later I came to know that all this was just a lie when I found out that she had left on the 6th of September itself. I kept stirring the warm coffee as the memory of how I felt when Mansi had accidentally burnt her finger flashed before my eyes. I was such a foolish chap! I thought that Mansi really loved me and thus devoted all my time and attention to her. I realized something—love is not at all a maze. It is the complicated people who make it seem complicated. Love is quite simple and innocent. I am not sad that I loved Mansi; rather, I am proud that I could love someone so deeply from the core of my heart. I had learnt that things do not always unfold the way we want them to, and that is why we feel sad. Everything in the world is a blessing and happens for a reason. Moreover, I might not have Mansi with me in person, but I will always have her in my heart till I die. But even after all these self-realisations, I did feel a bit sad when Mansi did not even wish me on my birthday. Perhaps, things had changed completely from the way they had been in the past, and I was still in a dream or a dilemma.

Yes, it might seem like a mistake on my part. But, honestly, I am proud that I did make the mistake. It is important to love and to feel loved. Because without love, life is but an empty dream.

You can end the story here and skip to the 'Reflection' if you like.

Otherwise, you are free to continue!

Life Equals Metamorphosis

The challenge was quite simple: I had to forget about Mansi and concentrate on my own life. But with time, things were getting harder for me. I could not sleep properly at night, could not concentrate on my work, and the memories of the past kept haunting me again and again. This is what happens when you face a mishap in your life. Whenever I tried to forget about Mansi, all those intimate moments spent with her flashed before my eyes and made situations more difficult for me. In my endeavour to get rid of my past, I got help form a Bollywood movie, *Bhaag Milkha Bhaag*[26], which I watched about twenty times or even more.

But even after trying a lot of different things, I failed to make myself understand that everything was over and that I had to move on. It is very easy to stand and comment on such things from a third person's perspective, but it is extremely difficult to get over something so deeply linked to your life. My performance at the office was on a steep decline, and thus my manager called me one day. He said, "Manav, what is the matter? I can feel that you are going through something. What is it? Tell me..." I did

---

[26] This is a true story of `the Flying Sikh' - world champion runner and Olympian Milkha Singh who overcame the massacre of his family and the civil war during the India-Pakistan partition

not want to disclose anything and thus said, "Sir, it's very personal. I don't want to disclose anything right now." He understood the problem and suggested me to take a few days of leave. He said, "Manav, take a leave and go somewhere. It will refresh you." The suggestion was not that bad, and I thought of giving it a try. I said, "Alright sir... It's better that I take a leave."

"It's alright, Manav. But for how many days do you want to be on leave?"

"I don't know, sir. The day I want to re-join, I will inform you."

"But there are some protocols that you must follow, Manav."

"Sir, I am not at all feeling well. I will talk to you later."

"Alright, take care of yourself." I took a leave of one year then.

I know that one year sounds like an unrealistic time frame to be on leave from office, but I had accumulated a lot of holidays, and moreover, I never expected that I would return to the post again after that.

I stopped going to office and started making plans for a trip. I changed my personal contact number, and even my home number. I deleted all my social network ID's on Twitter, Facebook, Instagram and the like. I stopped talking to and contacting anyone in my friend circle, and this went on for the next few months. The same old schedule and the same people were making it very hard for me to get over my past, and I needed a really long break. I tried a lot more things and explored a lot more areas.

After some time, I thought of consulting a clinical psychologist. I straightaway googled for the best psychologist in Delhi. The name of a lady popped up. She resided in South Delhi. I called her up and fixed an appointment for the next week.

It was on a Tuesday that I was to visit her at her clinic. I woke up early and got ready. I hired an auto till South Delhi and reached her clinic, which was on the ground floor of the lady's home itself. It was very well maintained. There was greenery all around; antique sculptures decorated almost every corner. The floor was finished with a Kashmiri carpet, on which were was a large, L-shaped sofa and carved wooden chairs. The wallpapers on all four walls and the two chandeliers on the ceiling made the entire room look really beautiful.

She offered me coffee, which I gently accepted. After that, the chit-chat began. I told her everything that had happened and what was going on in my mind. I shared all my destructive thoughts too. She took all my details and told me that I would have to visit her at least 7-8 times. She wanted to know everything in detail. She took around 2-3 hours on that day and kept writing everything I said in her notebook. Almost 20-25 pages!

I visited her about 4-5 times, but on my third visit she told me to bring one of my close friends with me. Actually, she wanted to confirm everything before coming to any conclusion.

I called Deepak immediately and told him about this. Though he was aware of everything about my past, he was initially a little cautious. But after I convinced him, he supported my decision and was ready to help me. He told me that next week he would be coming to Delhi from where he had a connecting flight to Bangalore. So, he would eventually meet me.

I don't know how, but after each visit to her clinic, I started to regain my lost confidence. I started liking the ambience there and my conversations with her. This process continued for the next 2-3 months. On my last visit, she asked me to do a few things afterwards. They were nothing special. She just asked me to go for a long drive without my mobile phone, listen to music, do night-outs, plan a holiday with my best friends to some hilly area, go on long, late-night walks in Lutyens Delhi, etc.

It was around this time that I developed the habit of listening to music. I also took to painting. Things were going good, but I was reminded of Mansi once again when I saw the calendar and realized that Mansi's birthday was approaching. In the depths of my heart, I was somehow still attached to her, and her birthday was still a special occasion for me. You know, we are wired in such a way that our body has a biological clock within. No matter how hard one tries to make things normal again, there are certain times when certain feelings are bound to resurface automatically. Thus, instead of running away from my weakness, I decided to face it. After her last birthday, which had been on the 21st of February, 2013, things had changed rapidly, and thus I wanted to celebrate her upcoming birthday like never before. I started all the preparations from two months before, and took care of each and every minute thing. To make things more special, I called up a bakery in Dehradun and ordered a delicious chocolate cake. I knew that Mansi loved chocolate cakes, and thus I wanted her to have a chocolate cake on her birthday. I started my journey early in the morning on the 21st of February, 2014. On the way, I took lots of photographs of my journey from Delhi to Dehradun. When I reached there, I took photographs of her locality, the streets, and her home. Mansi's mother was waiting for me. I had already informed her about my visit the previous day. I reached, and she greeted me and took me to her drawing room. Everything was the same as the last time I had been there. But there was one new addition: I found the collage which I had gifted Mansi after her Amity convocation hanging on the wall...Her mother asked me a few things about my work and family condition and I replied as honestly as I could. When she came to know that I had arranged for the cake, she asked me the reason for ordering such a big cake, upon which I remained silent. The drawing room had changed a lot. The walls had all been repaired and redone, and new photographs adorned them. The collage which I had given Mansi after the convocation was one of them. There was a small picture of me too in that photo, and when Akhilesh had asked Mansi regarding my photo being on that collage, she had said that I was one of her favourite professors! Mansi's mother came and offered me a cup of tea, and I bluntly refused to take it. She requested me to have a cup of coffee instead, and I said that I would not take anything. Her mother became disappointed and said, "If you will not drink even a glass of water in our house, then why did you bring such a big cake for Mansi?" I could no longer resist her insistent words and thus accepted to have a cup of coffee. After having the coffee, her mother handed over a small sum of money to me and said that she was giving that to me because on every birthday, she gave a little to her daughter. But Mansi was abroad and thus she wanted me to keep that sum of money. I could not resist this time and thus accepted it. I had prepared my gift for Mansi: the photo-frame with a picture of that bench outside her hostel where she used to sit and wait every day for me to come and pick her up. I placed my present on the tea-table and walked outside to my car. I was about to leave when her mother came outside and said, "Drive safe!" I could never fathom the reason for that gratitude. But that day, I really felt good. It was after a long time that I smiled and then drove home safely.

I re-joined my office after nearly a year. Everyone was annoyed with me, but nobody could express things directly. The most satisfying thing was that I was feeling refreshed and had recovered that long-lost energy. Everyone was happy to see me in such a jolly mood, and some of my workmates had even gotten a return gift for me. Things had really changed in one year, and I never could believe that I had been happily accepted into the job again after taking such a long leave. Just as I was about to settle down on my chair, the manager called for me and I had to leave. When I walked into his office, I found him smiling. He wished me a good morning and said, "Manav, there is a corporate fair going on just 10 km from here. We basically exhibit our latest technology, software and products there. I want you to attend it because it is right at the heart of the city and quite close to your residence." Although I did not feel like going, I had to because I could not refuse him after talking such a long leave from office. Thus, I drove my car to the fair. Since it was a corporate fair, I had to fill up some forms and submit them before entering. I was a bit late, and thus had to stand in along queue for the form. However, the place was not stuffy, and one could easily stand there for a couple of hours with ease. I decided to put on my headphones and listen to some music. As I was about to press the play button, I felt a soft pat on my shoulders. I turned back and found a girl asking me for help. She had some trouble understanding some details in the form, and thus asked me if I could take a look at it once. I was a bit annoyed with that sudden, unexpected disturbance but decided to help her fill out the form so that she would not disturb me any further. After the Mansi episode, I had been staying away from girls who were stranger, and had been actively avoiding any sort of interaction with them. I took the leaflet and clarified her doubts. She was pleased at having filled her form completely, and said to me, "Thank you very much! So how long will you be staying here?"

"Well, I don't know; maybe two to three hours."

"Well, can you please do something for me?"

"Well, until I know what help you need, I can't promise to help you."

"Ok! So can you submit my form along with yours, please?"

I was not at all sure why I was helping her. But I saw no harm in submitting her form along with mine because even if I did not help her, I would still have to stand in the queue and submit my form. Thus, I said that I would submit her form and told her to wait there till I returned. Unfortunately, just before it was my turn to submit the forms, it was declared that the capacity had become full and no more forms would be accepted. I was highly disturbed with this flawed system and went back to hand over the form to that girl. But when I reached that place, I could not find her anymore. I thought of dumping her profile in the nearby dustbin, but then thought of keeping it with me so that I could contact her later and give the form back to her.

I returned to the office and explained to the manager the whole story of the sudden cessation of form acceptance. He was furious with the fair officials and requested me to go home. When I returned home, there were a lot of guests. The family members of my cousin had come that day to invite us to a ring ceremony that was to be held within a week. I was slowly starting to forget my past and, having the constant company of my family members, I was getting back my lost happiness. I did not have the fear of losing someone anymore, and that was a real blessing for me.

I had work on the day of my cousin's ring ceremony, and thus I was a bit late and could not see the ring exchange properly. However, I went to the occasion and took a lot of photographs with various members of my family as well as the relatives, and was slowly sipping some warm coffee when suddenly, I felt the same pat on my shoulder. I turned around only to find that same girl who had requested me to submit her form. She looked very jolly that day and said to me, "Hey! How are you?"

"Well... I am good; enjoying my cousin's ring ceremony here. What about you? How come you are here?" I asked.

"So he is your cousin?" she asked.

"Yes," I said, "But you?"

"Actually, Payal, the girl whom your cousin is going to marry, is a resident of my society."

"Ohh... anyway, what's up??"

"Hmn, I am getting bored."

"Wao! It's really an achievement to get bored in such an occasion."

"Oh...really?"

"Yes...I hope so. And yes, it's good that you have come today. I wanted to return your form on that day, but you left. It has been with me since we last met."

Ahh! I don't need that anymore. You may throw it away. Actually that day, I got to know that no more forms were being accepted and thus I went away. I searched for you a lot but could not find you."

"Hmn, I searched for you too."

"So, what is your name?'

"I am Manav."

"Hmn, I am Rhea."

"What did you say? Rhea?"

"Yes, any problem?"

"No, actually it's a very good name."

"Well, thank you for that compliment."

"That was not a compliment. It's the truth."

"Ok...whatever... So, you live here?"

"Well, yes. I live here with my parents and our uncle used to live here along with us, but we split due to some differences."

"Hmn..."

"What about you? Don't you live here?"

"Yes, I live here, but my actual house in Calcutta. I have been living here for the last 12 years."

"Hmn, that's a long time."

"Yes, my parents have been living here fora long time. I love Delhi. But Calcutta is closer to my heart."

"Well Rhea, that's quite obvious because you were born and brought up there."

"Yes...it's some special link."

"Hmn..."

"So for how long are you going to stay here?"

"I don't know. Maybe I will leave right now. It all depends on my parents."

"Hmn... It was nice talking to you."

"My pleasure..."

"So, are you active on any social network?"

"Yes, I used to be, but now I am not."

"Hmn...That's good."

"Wait...I am on Facebook."

"What is your username?"

"My real name and profile name are both the same."

"Well, I shall send you a friend request then."

"Yes, sure..."

"Ok, bye. See you later."

"Yes, bye."

After a few minutes, I went home too. The ceremony had been a little exhausting for me, and thus I took a nap. After waking up, I took out my laptop and started working on an office project. After working for nearly three hours, I felt exhausted and thus switched to Facebook. Rhea had sent me a friend request and I accepted it. She was online and we started talking. Although I did not want to talk to her, I had no other creative work and thus thought of spending some time talking to her.

"So, what are you doing?"

"Nothing...just surfing through some profiles."

"Whose profile?"

"Some new friend's profile."

"Ooo..."

"What is this 'Ooo'?"

"Nothing..."

"So, when did you leave from the ceremony?"

"Just fifteen minutes after you."

"Hmn... So what are you doing now?"

"Nothing much, just working on some new project."

"Alright then... I won't disturb you anymore."

"You did not start a conversation at all. So how would you be disturbing me?"

"That does not matter. There is no first and last in a conversation. If you have work, then you can do it."

"No...Yes, I do have some work but I am bored now. I have been working for the last three hours."

"Oh, that's good. You have time then..."

"Yes."

"So, do you like talking to me?"

"Yes...I do."

"Why do you?"

"I don't know, maybe because you are the only one who is talking to me right now."

"What does that even mean?"

"It means that I just like that you are talking to me because you are the only one talking to me."

"Well, whatever..."

"Hmn..."

"So, when do you go to sleep?"

"There is really no fixed time. However, I go to sleep at around twelve on average."

"Hmn. So two hours more to go."

"Yes. Two hours before I go to sleep."

"Hey, can I have your number?"

"Why?"

"No, I mean, if you have some problem then no need."

"No, actually I don't have any problem."

"So, what is your number?"

"It's there in my profile's contact section. Wait, I am making it public for now."

"Yes...got it."

"That's good..."

Just then, my phone buzzed. It was a missed call from Rhea. I noted her number and saved it in my contact list under the name, "Mysterious stranger." I was feeling sleepy and thus said, "Hey...I am feeling sleepy."

"Ok...Good night then."

"Yes...Good night."

The next morning, when I woke up, I found that I had five missed calls from Rhea. I washed my face, got ready for office, and then called her. She picked up and asked me in a jolly voice, "Good morning, Sir. What are you doing?" I was in a hurry and thus replied, "Good morning. I am leaving for work." She laughed and then replied, "Yes... Best of luck!" I got surprised and asked, "What's so funny about that?" She kept laughing and then replied, "It's nothing. Reach safe. And yes, make sure that you drive carefully. Or else, I am pretty sure that you will bump into some vehicle and then the driver will accuse me for not telling you to be careful." This reply made me nostalgic and brought out all the emotions of the past. I wanted to meet her and thus said, "Are you free today evening?" She said that she would make some time for me and we agreed to meet at a cafe.

I could not understand why, but that day, I had a tough time concentrating on my work. I opened up her profile and went through her photos. All this seemed so surreal to me and I tried hard to restrict myself from getting into such thoughts again. I did not want to repeat the same mistake twice, and thus called her and cancelled that day's plan. She was a bit upset with that because she had somehow made time for me, and I cancelled the whole plan at the very last moment. Although I cancelled the plan, I decided to spend that same time chatting with her. Thus, I took out my laptop, opened Facebook and sent her a "Hello!" She was offline and I thought of calling her, but did not. So I waited for another thirty minutes and then when my patience ran out, I called her. She was in her house, and came online within a minute. I did not know why, but I felt happy talking to her.

I started finding her voice soothing and kept talking to her for some time. She made me feel happy. Finally, I told her all about Mansi and our relationship and she felt sad for me. She said that sometimes in life we need to give up some things to understand the way of life, and these words rang completely true for me. I could not resist myself, and within a few months, I had gotten close to her. That feeling, which had destroyed my mind and my heart, came back again, only this time, to heal me and fill my inner self with inexplicable happiness. Rhea was her name, and I had fallen for her.

Although we both understood that we had feelings for each other, we were waiting for the other to take the first step. I was too busy with my work and thus did not get the time to meet her at a proper place. One fine evening, I called Deepak, who was posted in Ambala then, and told him everything regarding Rhea. He could not understand at first and confused Rhea with Mansi. But after hearing closely, he understood everything and became very happy. The following evening, he came to my house and we had a nice chat regarding life and work. Finally, I got a day off and decided to meet Rhea in a nearby Coffee Cafe Day outlet. She came wearing a white dress, and was looking beautiful that day. There was something very strange about the two of us. We could talk for hours on social media and over call, but whenever we met each other face-to-face, neither of us could to talk to the other freely. However, I was very confident that day. After we took our respective seats, I handed her the menu card and requested her to order anything she would like to have. She ordered two coffees. Then, I came closer to her and said, "I wanted to tell you something very special." She blushed and said, "I already know." Hearing this, I smiled, and then taking her left hand in my palm, gave her the ring. She was amazed on seeing it and hugged me tight. I felt true love for the first time, and after nearly two years uttered the words, "I love you," again. She kissed me on my cheeks and said, "I love you too." And then we sat together sipping the warm coffee and talking about some important things. Rhea said, "My parents have been pressurizing me about my marriage. After going home today, I am going to tell them about us."

"Yes. And I will also tell my parents about us."

"We are going to get married soon, mister! I like you so much."

"Acchaa... and what if I say that I don't love you?"

"Haha... you would never say that."

"Why not?"

"Because I know that you won't. My heart says that you won't."

"I think we should give ourselves some more time."

"Yes, I totally agree with you. But I really can't understand the hurry of my parents."

"Seriously, this life is ours, but I can't figure out why parents are more keen about our marriage than us."

"Yes! It feels as if they are going to achieve something great by getting us married."

"Hmn. Perhaps they want to settle things altogether."

"Whatever...so I am telling my parents about us tonight itself."

"Hmn...me too."

"Let's go now. It's getting late."

"Alright, let's go."

Thus, we went outside and I drove her to her house. Before getting out from my car, she said that she was going to be with me for the rest of her life. I wished her Good night.

It was the second week of February, and things slowly started to brighten up. Rhea's maternal grandfather was a very good friend of my father, and thus things became really easy for the both of us. My parents did not want to delay things and neither did hers. Before I could know, the date of my engagement with Rhea was fixed in the month of April. Everyone in my office got happy after hearing this, and my close friends congratulated me on such good news. We were to get married in December, and I started calling everybody one by one to invite them to my marriage.

It was 10:00 p.m. (IST) when I called Akhilesh and asked him to give the phone to Mansi. Unfortunately, he was travelling to some place that day and so could not hand over the phone to Mansi. Nevertheless, I informed him about my marriage and invited him to attend the party. He expressed no emotion after hearing the news (I don't know what impression Mansi had created of me in front of him), but he congratulated me. He promised that he would try to attend the auspicious occasion and wished me good luck for the journey ahead. Next, I called Mansi's mother and told her about my marriage. She already knew about my engagement with Rhea, and had seen the pictures on social media. She congratulated me and said that I was lucky enough to get such a beautiful lady as my life-partner. I thanked her for saying so and invited her to my marriage. I also asked her to bring Mansi's younger sister, Shweta, to which she simply replied, "Hmn..." and then cut the call. I did not mind her attitude, and actually called her again to inform that I would send her the wedding card as well.

Finally, it was the 3rd of December—my wedding day. It was around 2:00 p.m., and all my family members had gone to the parlour to get themselves ready. Just then, my phone blared. I immediately recognized the number—it was Mansi's mother.

"Hello!"

"Hi Aunty..."

"Hi Manav... Congratulations."

"Thank you aunty, how are you?"

"I am good; how about you..."

"I am well too."

"Manav, I am sorry; I will not be able to attend your marriage ceremony."

I was astonished to hear that and asked, "Why aunty? What's the problem?"

She remained silent for some time and then started weeping. Her voice turned soft and in that soft voice, she said, "I am really sorry for whatever I did with you, Manav. But I was helpless. If Mansi was in your destiny, you would have surely gotten her. Regardless, in the next life, I promise you that with God's wishes, you will get her as your wife." I was dumbfounded after hearing that. But to avoid silence, I said, "Thank you so much aunty. It means a lot to me. But why will you not be able to come?" She had no reply to this question and, still sobbing, she just said "I am sorry, Manav" a couple more times and hung up. I could not understand her reason for not attending my marriage, and thus forgot about the conversation very soon.

Just as I was getting ready, I heard a knock on the door and started guessing who could be standing outside. I was sure that it was Deepak or someone from my office. Thus, I combed my hair and opened the door. I was taken aback by what I saw next. There was a fine man in a black suit who was standing at my doorstep, looking directly at me. I could not recognize him at first, but then his smile struck a lamp in my mind. I could not believe my eyes. It was Kartik! He was now the manager of some company. I could not control my emotions and thus went forward and hugged him tightly. He was very angry with me and said, "Did not even bother to inform me, huh?" I felt guilty and apologized to him a thousand times. Gifted with this reunion, my happiness knew no limits. Someone once rightly said that when life showers its happiness on us, we remain stunned. I had never expected Kartik to come, but he did not forget our friendship. The strong roots of emotions on which we had built our friendship were still fresh and alive. So, the marriage ceremony took place, and there was enjoyment all around.

Looking back at those days, I still cannot believe that so many things have happened. Maybe my mind stopped working the day I started loving Mansi. Maybe I am still stuck there, because it seems as if everything happened just last week. I still get depressed sometimes, and still keep asking the same old questions: why did Mansi leave me, and whether at all she loved me through those months or not. I do not know whether I have completely moved on or not. But I think it is quite impossible for me to forget Mansi, on whose palm I had carved myself.

A few days passed. I was in the marriage party of a friend, and one of my friends who knew about my relationship with Mansi informed me that she was expecting a baby. I was a bit shocked by this information as I had thought that Mansi would tell me the news first. I had called her mother a couple of days back, but she also had not told me anything regarding this. Nevertheless, I prayed for a long and prosperous life for the baby and remembered the promise I had made to Mansi.

When I had met Mansi in her hometown, I promised her inside the Cafe Coffee Day shop that when she would give birth to her first baby, I would send her a hand-written poem. So, I wrote a poem that went like this:

Ek nanha munnah vanshaj dega sabke hotho par muskaan
Is kilkaari gunjan ke liye ishwar tumhe shat shat pranaam
Tum par barse amrat ban, jiwan ka har chhan har pal

Surya, chandrama, maathhe chamke, naina bane kamal
　　Tum par nyochaawar jo jag sara
Gun gayen har disha, dev, bhu, madhaya lok tumhara
　　Veer, tejasvi, satya ho tumhara har kathan,
Bharat garv kare dekar tumhe "Bharat Ratna"
　　Ujjwal bhavishey kare bhagya pradaan
Manav, mange yahi vardaan, yhi vardaan, yhi vardaan...

I placed the piece of paper with this poem inside a photo-frame and mailed it to her. I also dropped her an e-mail and messaged her on Facebook, but she did not reply. By now, I was used to her awkward silences, and no longer waited for her reply. Life is a great teacher. It not only stuffs us with information, but also involves us in the learning process. After everything that had happened, I had come to learn that life is really like a bicycle, and that we must always pedal forward to maintain a steady balance.

Sometimes, when I look back, I still ask myself whether Mansi really loved me or not. If yes, then it was natural to have issues on the way, because every relationship on this planet has some or the other draw-back, and requires compromise somewhere. The thing of utmost priority is the love between two souls. Although there are rare cases where families have agreed in one go, I believe that the most important thing for a couple is to have faith and stand by each other during a maelstrom rather than to dump each other. I had blind faith in Mansi, and thought that she would never ever leave me. But she did not have the same feelings for me. Love means trust and respect, which rise above all materialistic factors like horoscope, customs, caste, etc. But amidst all these invisible storms, I still do care for her a lot, and will continue to help her in the future as a good friend whenever she is in need of me—anytime, anywhere. But whenever I close my eyes to take a break from my work and thoughts, my conscience comes rushing in and I feel like someone who has been used for good and then thrown away in the dirt.

Whenever I lose control over myself, I think of those sweet moments I had spent with Mansi. I am not ashamed that I loved Mansi. Although our relationship did not work out, it did gift me some precious moments which will remain in my mind till I die. There is not a single day when I do not think about Mansi. She is there with me in each and everything I do in my life. She is safe in my heart, and no one can make her go away from that place. Maybe I will never disclose whatever happened between us, but time shall know that I loved someone truly, and it is this thought which keeps me going in my life. Whenever I am upset, I sometimes call Mansi or her mom. After all this, I have no clue why I still feel the way I felt before. Mansi had once told me that she saw the reflection of her mom in me, and I think that is reason enough for me to feel the way I still do.

Now, I wait for the stars to play their miracle and I wait for another life; another fresh start where neither caste nor religion would be able to keep us apart. There would only be one priceless religion which would bind us together, and that religion would be '**love**.'

Reflection

Yes, the first time I saw her, I could have never imagined that I would fall for her. Isn't this the first line in every single person's love story? You never know that you are going to fall for someone, but then you actually do. Sometimes, normal people become so special that they leave a deep mark on the sands of your time.

She was also a normal girl after all. A batchmate, you might say. But it was love that made its way into my soul. Yes, love is that powerful. In my perspective, love is the single most powerful entity in the entire universe. It makes place for people in our hearts and teaches us to cherish the faults in ourselves, but most importantly, it turns something ordinary into something special.

Every single morning, I used to visit my garden and water my rose plants. It was a daily task, and there was nothing special about it. I used to wake up, go to my garden, and then water the plants. But one season, it so happened that I thought of observing how a small bud blooms into a rose. It was indeed a tedious process. Every evening, I used to sit with my cup of coffee and observe that small bud dancing in the wind. However, much of the process took place when I was not there. My wooden chair would remain there and wait for my arrival. After a few weeks, when I went to see the bud, I was already too late. The bud had long disappeared, leaving behind a full-bloomed rose. But what stunned me the most was that even though there were ten other roses on that plant, I could still distinguish between my rose and the other roses.

Yes, this is love. I had poured so much time and emotion into that one single flower that it had become a special flower for me.

So, we met...we talked...we got to know each other...we felt for each other, and then came the really hard choices. In fact, things were so overpowering that I could not help but feel helpless. Sometimes, you sense that something is not going right, but you still like to believe that everything is going to be fine.

It actually takes a lot of faith and courage to accept that what is lost shall never come back, and that some things are better left undone.

I had always been this studious guy, and actually, all that I had understood was that I needed to study hard and get good grades. Things are actually fine when you are under the impression that everything shall be taken care of. However, the irony is that everyone wants to become independent but nobody actually wants to take matters into their own hands.

So, I met her for the first time when our first term results were about to be released. She was standing there with bright eyes and a beautiful smile on her face. I still remember how she used to care about me. How she caressed me when I became hopeless. It was all meant to be.

After all this, it feels like things were always meant to be this way. As if it was only a story waiting to be told. But, sometimes, I do ask myself whether I had given all that I could or not, whether I did all that I could do or not. But these questions and all these reflections are useless now. The ability to differentiate between the essentials and the luxuries is what makes us sensible human beings. Yes, it takes time to move on from something. But the main thing to determine here is whether we should actually move on or not.

I was going through the translations of some English words in other languages, and I was quite overwhelmed to see that the word 'end' in Italian is 'fine' in English.

And so it should be. At the end, it is always fine. That is what matters. We humans are incredible creatures. We always try to arrange things in a logical sequence. Every single thing that we do in response to the things that happen to us, comes from our inner logic. And if you ask me even at this moment whether Manav was right or wrong, I would always say that he was right. Love is essential and inevitable. Anything that breathes on this planet or anywhere in this universe has at some point felt the touch of love.

After all, love is redemption. So, should I take a doctor's consultation to get rid of my past? The answer is quite simple. It's a big 'NO.' I am what I am because of what I was. And there are certain things which keep creating ripples even after they have ceased to exist. But if it becomes necessary to leave what is to be left, I shall never endeavour to cling onto it. Whatever the rest of the story is, time shall tell.

Epilogue

When you walk through this journey, be aware not to barter your priceless feelings with someone who takes them lightly and has no respect for them. Be careful not to look for harbours or ports nearby to rest your vessel when it is shattered by the strong winds at sea. Keep moving with the broken sails and wait for a miracle. Because, if you can maintain your faith under the toughest of conditions and have the courage to plunge into the depths of ocean even after knowing that there are no pearls down there, you will see a way through your darkness. You shall be amazed to see how things fall apart only to fall into the correct places and realize that life is a harmonic tune which keeps playing even if there is no audience to hear it. It keeps playing even if the sun is down and the nights are cloudy. You will never be able to understand how nature works and how life blends into this harmonious tune. There is a fine string which knits all of us together into one united sphere. The name of that string is love, and love is the source of all creation.

Love is like a rose. Although there are thorns that hurt, love is the only thing that keeps us alive and defies logic in its highest limits. So, when you sail out for your destination, make sure you get the maps clear and make arrangements for potential threats along the way. Don't hurry at all; move slowly along the way. And after you reach your destination, if you find that there is no treasure, then do not get upset, because the only treasure that the destination could offer you was the journey itself.

When you are in love, let not any external factors affect your relationship. Let trust, love and respect play their parts. Take care of your feelings and your partner too with whom you are in a relationship. A single choice from your side can have a huge impact in someone else's life. Let love slowly boil and release its unique flavours. Think and make sure you choose your words carefully. Make sure all your decisions come from the depths of your heart. It is important that you keep thinking about the mutual good and not just act like a selfish person.

After 31st of May 2012, even with all the complications, I was completely ready for a court marriage and even entirely willing to take the responsibility for the future of both of our families. But you did not agree on this.

There might have been a few mistakes from my side as well, but nothing as big as the one-sided decision you took.

Mansi, **"you were wrong on that day, and even today. But I still have respect for you and your decision. The time that we spent together was the best time of my life. Now, it is the time for the crown to pass from one hand to another."**

So, every story ends in reality. But mine did not. My story did start and end in fantasy because the reality was entirely different from her words and our so called 'love story.'

Jab Jab Dard Ka Badal chhaya
Jab jab gam ka saya lehraya
Jab aansoo palko tak aaya
Jab ye tanha dil ghabraya
Humne dil ko ye hi samjhaya
Dil akhir tu kyon rota hai
Duniya mein yu hi hota hai

Ye jo gehre sannate hai
Waqt ne sabko baaten hai
thoda gam ha sabka kissa
thodi dhoop hai sabka hissa
aankh teri bekaar hi nam hai
har pal ek naya mausam hai
kyu tu aise pal khota hai
dil akhir tu kyu rota hai
duniya mein yu hi hota hai

kyu tu yaad karta hai usko
fikar nhi thi teri jra bhi jisko
sunehri manjil ki thi jise talaash
bhujha na saka tu uski pyaas
manjhi, nhi thi vo tere kabil
na hi thi vo teri manjil

apne aapko pehchaan
le ab apni asli udaan
uske pechee…kyu tu sab khota hai
dil akhir tu kyu rota hai
duniya mein yu hi hota hai

… Literary genius Javed Akhtar Sahab,
recrafted by ..Akshat Jain

These lines are dedicated to...

Memories

Maa Saraswati Statue in front of the college entrance gate

College Campus

Tored Newspapers in the class, 2nd April 2008

Senior - Rashmi Priya

Satyam Placement drive at Dehradun

Satyam Placement at Dehradun. After being rejected in the 1st round, we all went to Mussoorie on 15 June 2007, Friday. 4:51 pm

All of us at one chopper

First SSB at 1AFSB Dehradun, 16 April 2008

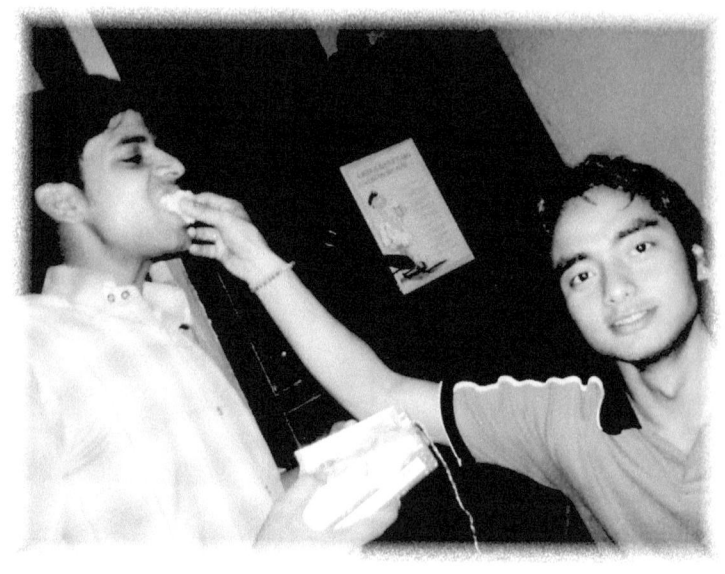

My Placement, 24th May 2008, Saturday

Placement Party in the campus

Last day of my college, Monday 2nd June 2008, 4:25 pm

Last Day in the college

Last Days

Last Days

Akshardhaam Temple, Delhi

Kalka Ji Temple, Delhi

My Royal Palace in College times

Second Home

Cafe Coffee Day

Place I'll never forget

Having pleasant time at DND Flyover

Amity Convocation 12th Dec 2012

More than a Friend - Deepak Yadav

My Inspirations - General Bipin Rawat & My Wife

*My childhood teacher and a great mathematician
Late Sh. R. K. Gupta Sir*

Blessings from Grand Pa & Grand Ma

About the Author

The author, Akshat Jain, was born and brought up in the province of Uttar Pradesh—the Sugar Bowl of India—in 1986. His education started in the best available convent school at that time in his hometown. Eventually, in 2004, he found his way to an engineering college and, over the protests of the school administration many times on different acts, he managed to annex a degree in engineering. He then infiltrated Amity University and BITS Pilani and climbed the academic ladder, completing his MBA & MS, ignoring all cries of outrage until he found himself well-settled in the corporate world and currently working at the Royal Bank of Scotland as Asst. Vice President. With the desire to do something more, he is actively working as a political analyst and strategist in one of the country's biggest political parties.

Now, in the second phase of his life, the author has sobered up (or has been trying to) and has undertaken the noblest mission one could think of—giving back to the society for the betterment of future generations. For this, he makes use of his fluid way with words and weaves narratives around topics that a young audience would eagerly lap up. In all seriousness, the underlying purpose of his literary works has always been to support and aid social causes. He derives inspiration from his wife, family, friends, and belated friends.

When he's not in his usual frenzy, he loves to sit down and watch the news and shows on Discovery.

Please share your feedback

✉ *akshat@akshatjain.org.in*

🐦 *writer_akshat*

📷 *writer_akshat*

www.ingramcontent.com/pod-product-compliance
Ingram Content Group UK Ltd.
Pitfield, Milton Keynes, MK11 3LW, UK
UKHW042003230426
12048UKWH00009B/522